CITY OF DECEPTION

BARSOOM II
OUTLAWED COLONIES 8

GAIL DALEY

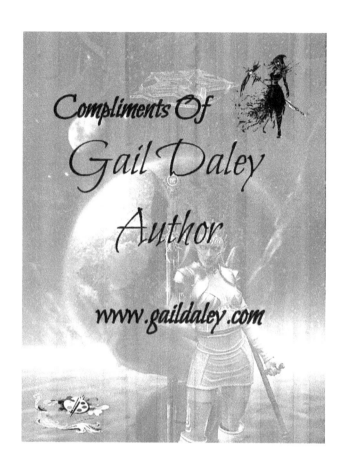

Compliments Of

Gail Daley

Author

www.gaildaley.com

GAIL'S OTHER BOOKS

SPACE COLONY JOURNALS
Options of Survival
Destiny Rising
Tomorrows Legacy
The Interstellar Jewel Heist
The Designer People
Alien Trails
Quantum Light

NEXT GENERATION SPACE COLONY JOURNALS
Soturi! *

ABOUT GAIL'S WORLDS

Federation Colonies & Civilizations
Rulari - Land of Myth & Magic
Forbidden & Outlawed

ST. ANTONI - THE FORBIDDEN COLONY

Warriors of St. Antoni
The Enforcers
The Gaslight Bandits
Cradle of Fire

GAIL DALEY'S DYSTOPIAN EARTH

The Portal Lawman
The Clone Initiative
Cloned Ambition

Gail Daley

THE OUTLAWED COLONIES

Game Theory
Heirs of Avalon
Apex Predator
Babylon Shattered
The Arcadian Web
Daughter of Shadows
City of Deception
Riddle of the Halivaara Wheel*
Day of the Clone*

MAGI OF RULARI TRILOGY

Spell of The Magi
Magi Storm
Paladin

NON-FICTION

The Complete Modern Artist's
Handbook

PAMPHLETS

Introduction to The Internet #1
The Hard Stuff - Handbook #2
Art Show Basics - Handbook #3
Framing on a Budget - Handbook #4
Are You Making Money? - Handbook #5
For Writers Only - Handbook #6*

*Working Title. Release dates TBA

COPYRIGHT

e-book ISBN: 9798886272840
Print book ISBN: 9781684891849

ASIN:
For permission requests, write to the publisher, addressed "Attention: Permissions Coordinator," at the address below.

Gail Daley
5688 E Sussex Way
Fresno, CA 93727
www.gaildaley.com

Ordering Information: Quantity sales. Special discounts are available on quantity purchases by corporations, associations, and others. For details, contact the "Bulk Sales Department" at the address above.

Publisher's Note: This is a work of fiction, and any resemblance to any persons living or dead is unintentional and accidental.

Names, characters, places, and incidents are a product of the author's imagination. Locales and public names are sometimes used for atmospheric purposes. Any resemblance to actual people, living or dead, or to businesses, companies, events, institutions, or locales is completely coincidental.

ABOUT THIS BOOK

Welcome to the mysterious colony of Barsoom where the colonists kept the romance of the Renaissance but paired it with advanced technology.

When a teenage girl goes missing, the peaceful facade is shattered, and three couples are thrown into a dangerous web of criminal activity. The last person she was seen with was the sinister Jean Coudet, a member of the notorious Red Conclave.

Devon Morten and Tash Higgins, returning to the colony for their friends' wedding, never expected to be caught up in a race against time. Along with their friends Randal and Judith, Judith's older sister Ava and the girl's father Carlos, they must navigate the treacherous underbelly of the colony to find the missing girl before it's too late.

If you enjoy books filled with an exciting blend of technology. Intrigue, mystery, danger, and a touch of romance, then you'll love City of Deception.

Table of Contents

GAIL'S OTHER BOOKS 3
COPYRIGHT 5
ABOUT THIS BOOK 8
FEEL THE RYTHEM 12
LONG ARM OF THE LAW 27
WALKING THE LINE 34
CLOSE TO MIDNIGHT 48
MIDNIGHT FRENZY 62
THE MAN IN THE IRON MASK 73
NIGHT HUNTER 77
THE COLD HAND OF DARKNESS 93
EVIL IS AS EVIL DOES 106
AT SWORDS POINT 120
MOTHER BEAR 131
RIDE THE MAN DOWN 151
MEDEA'S CHOICE 165
DAUGHTER OF DARKNESS 175
RUN, FOX RUN 186
GIRL'S DAY OUT 201
HUNTING THE BEAR 221
YOU ARE MY HEARTBEAT 230
BATTLE LINES 245
THE 12TH OF NEVER 262
THE COLONY OF BARSOOM* 282

    HISTORY. 282
    GENERAL DESCRIPTION. 285
    GEOGRAPHICAL FEATURES. 288
        GREAT RAINBOW MOUNTAINS. 289
        PARCHESTER RIVER. 289
        LANGSTINO SEA. 290

    SOCIAL VALUES AND MANNERS. 291
        CODE DUELLO. 292

    ANIMALS. 295
        LINT DRAGON: 295
        CATAMOUNT: 296
        HAIRY CATAMOUNT: 297

KEVLAR: 298
GREYHOUND DEER 299
HERMIT FLYER 300
WHISPS: 301

PLANTS 301
COLONIAL SETTLEMENTS 302
CAPITAL CITY: SAVONA 303
ROSEWOODS PLANTATION 304
DANCING BEACH 305

TECH LEVEL 306

ABOUT THE AUTHOR 308
A NOTE FROM GAIL 311
GAME THEORY 314
HEIRS OF AVALON 316
APEX PREDATOR 318
BABYLON SHATTERED 320
THE ARCADIAN WEB 322
CLONED AMBITION 324
DAUGHTER OF SHADOWS 326
PALADIN 328
QUANTUM LIGHT 330
COMING IN 2025 332

FEEL THE RYTHEM

AVA GARNEYS checked the display on her tablet against the survey marker she had just inserted into the ground to ensure it was securely placed. This was the last marker she needed to set today. Satisfied, she swung an armored-clad leg over the seat of her personal airsled and headed back to base camp. Ava was a mapmaker and explorer attached to the Outlawed Colony of Barsoom. She was the last one to return to base today.

"There you are girl. I was beginning to think we needed to send out search parties," Mathilde Dale, a petit blond and one of her fellow mapmakers chided as Ava slid her airsled into its customary place outside the Pop-up dome they shared with the other female member of the team, Thomasine Willys, who was busily preparing tonight's meal. Thomasine was about medium height with a chunky body and light brown hair which she wore in a short bob for easier care and maintence out in the field.

"Not likely," Ava retorted before disappearing into their dome to shed the armor she wore during the day, re-emerging in the leggings and sweatshirt she customarily wore when off duty. Ava had inherited her height and lanky build from her father as well as his ginger hair.

"I leave for town tomorrow, remember?" she said.

"Yeah, a month off to laze around and try on clothes," Constantine

Bryan, one of the two male members of the team and the only one who looked the part of the intrepid explorer, said.

"I see you've never been at ground zero during the weeks before a wedding," hooted Jacques Brunelle, a tall, skinny nerd. "I remember when my sister got married! Ordinarily she's okay for a sister—but talk about turning into Bridzilla! Ava'll probably want to come back here to relax!"

"Now that Ava's back, we can turn on the security field," Constantine announced, staring pointedly at Jacques.

"I did it last night. It's your turn," Jacques told him.

"We need to redo next month's chore rotation, anyway," Mathilde who was senior stated. "We'll do that after dinner, so don't anyone run off immediately."

"Yeah, the deserter here will be gone for a month," Constantine said.

Ava sank into her customary camp chair, stretching her long legs out toward the Crystal heater. "You're breaking my heart, Bud," she snorted.

Compared to down near Savona, the colony's capital city, which nestled in the hot and humid tropic zone, it was chilly up here in the mountains, especially at night. She would be glad of her insulated sleeping bag later.

When she left the next morning, dawn was just breaking. The twin moons could still be seen in the sky and the rising sun had turned the horizon a splendid orange, fading into lavender, and then into the dark blue of night.

Jacques had been right, damn him—she wasn't looking forward to the weeks before her baby sister's wedding. Judith was marrying Randal Langton, the son of one of her dad's business partners, who she had been affianced to since they were children. The marriage was an arrangement between their parents, as was the custom in the colony which adhered as closely as possible with the way things had been done in the Renaissance.

They would have done the same for Ava; indeed, they tried—but she had been singularly uncooperative. She had managed to torpedo all the arrangements her parents tried to make for her. Gossip and innuendo had done the rest. No one wanted to try and marry their son to her. Ava was glad for Judith, but she knew she was going to have to endure the humiliation of her parents looking for a husband for her among the wedding guests and any single young men of the right age. The trouble was her taste and that of her parents simply didn't fit well together.

Her unpleasant thoughts were interrupted by a fracas going on below her. Swooping lower on her sled, she saw several Kevlar had cornered what looked like a furry catamount. Why didn't the silly creature simply climb the tree behind her to get away? She wondered. Then she spotted the litter of pups half-hidden under the bush next to the tree.

Kevlars were a Medium to large carnivore, with shaggy, green mottled fur, pointed ears and Predator eyes. After an incident earlier in the year when someone had attempted to kidnap Judith, her new brother-in-law to be had insisted on installing some weapons on their personal sleds. He had done Ava's first since she intended to leave as soon as her

17

father had been cleared, but for some reason had put off adding weapons to Judith's personal sled. Ava suspected this was because Randal didn't want his fiancée to go looking for trouble.

Ava squeezed the handlebars and a plasma bolt shot out, clipping the rear of the Kevlar pack. With a squeal of rage and fright, they ran away. They would be back, she knew. Kevlar's were hunters; they might have been frightened away, but the pack would soon overcome their fear and return.

The Catamounts found around Savona were nearly hairless an evolutionary adaption to the heat, but this one had a short, dense coat of golden fur fading to white around the paws and face. Intending to document the creature, she stopped her sled close to the tree, dissolved the wind-blocking force bubble over the sled and pulled out her vid-cam to take pictures. Up close the resemblance to a Catamount was even more pronounced. The skin under the dense fur was still wrinkled. Either this was a previously unknown variant or an entirely new species. The colonists had only been in residence on Barsoom for about 150 years; there was a lot they didn't know about their new planet.

The mother was thin to the point of emancipation, and she was weakening rapidly. Ava dismounted her sled and crouched in front of the dying animal. Cautiously she reached out to touch the kits. The first three she touched were dead, cold and stiff, but one of them was moving, attempting to nurse, even though it was plain her mother had no milk to feed her. When Ava touched the kit, the mother hissed feebly and then

19

simply closed her eyes and died. Ava gently slid a hand under the live kit and lifted it. It was cold but still alive. She tucked it inside her shirt, next to her skin and re-mounted her sled. She could see the Kevlar pack peeking out at her from across the clearing, and hastily hit the lift button on the sled. It wasn't unknown for a Kevlar pack to attack a lone human on the ground or even one on a one-man sled like hers if it was flying low enough. She re-instated the force bubble and gunned the engine. Behind her she could hear the Kevlar fighting among themselves for the corpses of the dead creatures.

In town, her first stop was the veterinarian used by her sister for Licorice, her pet Catamount.

Like Ava, Dr. Helewis Peele was tall, with short-cropped dark hair and a fit body. She looked up as Ava gently removed the animal from inside her shirt and laid her on the examining table. "A Hairy Catamount!" she exclaimed. "Wherever did you find it?"

"A pack of Kevlars were fighting her mom as I passed over on the way home. I scared them away with a plasma bolt across their tails and they ran. The mom died in front of me. This was the only kit still alive. I couldn't leave her there to die or be eaten, so I brought her with me."

"Was she still nursing?"

"Well, she was trying to, but I doubt if the mom had any milk. She was awfully skinny."

Dr. Peele nodded. She ran a scanning wand over the small animal. "Female, about three weeks old. We'll put her on a formula we use for

Catamounts. I take it you're planning to adopt her?"

"I guess so," Ava said, feeling a tug on her heartstrings. She's a fighter."

"What are you going to name her?"

Ava looked down at the small body with its dense golden fur, fading into white around her face and paws. "Sunrise, for the time I found her."

"I'll send a vet-bot with nursing supplies and a few other things I think you will need over to your house. In the meantime, just keep her warm and her tummy full." She handed Ava a half full glass bottle with a nipple and showed her how to get the kit to drink. Sunrise latched on fiercely, swallowing nearly the entire bottle, after which she burped and went to sleep.

Ava looked up with a smile. "I guess she was hungry."

On the way home from the vets, she stopped off at a local pet store and purchased a pet bed, some food dishes and litter box supplies which she had sent to her parents' home.

The house her father had built for their mother was just the same as she remembered; a 3-story edifice nestled on the water, with the bottom floors open to the air, with tall trees, whose enormous broad leaves shaded the house from the sun and heat, rising around it. She parked her sled on the deck where two robot servers waited for her.

"Welcome home, Miss Ava," the one in the butler's livery said. "How was your trip home?"

"A little exciting Marston," she told the senior robot. Even though the servers were only robots, Tamara Garneys demanded her family address them as if they were real people.

23

"Dr. Peele will be sending over a vet bot and a few essential items for my new Catamount. My clothes and stuff are in the saddle bags and side storage."

She extracted Sunrise from inside her shirt. The small animal blinked still blurry eyes at him.

"He has fur," Marston said, his robot voice showing surprise. Most robots on Barsoom had been programmed to interact with humans as their programing dictated another human would.

"Yes, she is a different variety than Licorice," Ava replied referring to her sister Judith's pet, whose fine, transparent hair revealed his nearly blue-black skin.

She had no chance to say more; Judith and Tamara became impatient for her to come inside and rushed out. Judith showed her inheritance from her parents as clearly as Ava did, she resembled their mother, except for her flame-tinged hair. Ava had always felt her sister looked like one of the fairies in the stories Tamara liked to read to them as children. She was tiny, like their mother, with the same Rubenesque figure. Tamara's once voluptuous figure had softened into matronly lines, and her hair, once a platinum blond, was now simply white.

"Ava!" Judith cried, throwing her arms around her sister to hug her.

"Careful! You'll squash Sunrise," Ava exclaimed in her turn.

Judith drew back. "Oh, what is it?"

"She's a catamount, like Licorice, but a different variety. Dr. Peele called her a Hairy Catamount."

"What an ugly name for such a sweet-looking creature," Tamara had given her daughter a much gentler hug. Now she stroked a finger over the kit's tiny head.

"Come inside and let's get you and Sunrise settled in your room. We're having some friends over for tea later. I've laid out some fresh clothes for you. All you need to do is take a shower and freshen up."

Ava sighed. The wedding circus was starting already. "Who's coming?"

"Oh, the usual crowd." Judith answered.

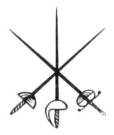

LONG ARM OF THE LAW

BARSOOM WAS a planned colony. Part of the planning had included creating a court system. Although the Colonists deeply admired the Renaissance lifestyle, they hadn't hesitated to alter customs where they considered changes necessary. Although it paid a small stipend, the job of Chief prosecutor and his subordinates was voluntary. After the volunteers had put in their names for consideration they were reviewed and selected by a judicial council every three years. This was how Carlos Santana had come to serve as a prosecutor. He had been selected over the other candidates because although he was now a solid family man, he had a history of being a tough opponent who didn't scare easily. In his younger days he had been a famous duelist, an excellent shot with a pistol, and a master of bladed weapons. The Black Templars and the judicial committee were aware that he had also been a bounty hunter before he took up the law as a profession.

Carlos Santana was tall and slender with finely cut features and melting chocolate eyes behind absurdly long eyelashes. His dark hair had just enough grey in it to give his handsome looks a distinguished air.

Just now he was prosecuting a case against Christopher Moyet who was believed to be an enforcer for the Red Conclave, a local criminal organization, for extortion. It was a solid case and Carlos was confident of a guilty verdict. A series of alternate threats and bribes offered hadn't stopped him from forging ahead. That morning before court had convened, he found his clerk, Denis Norward, a rotund little man with limp brown hair, attempting to dispose of an envelope without giving it to his boss.

"You needn't be afraid to show it to me Denis," Carlos held out his hand for the envelope. "What part of my anatomy am I going to lose this time?"

Denis turned stricken eyes to his boss. "It isn't about you sir," he said, watching Carlos open the envelope. Several vid-stills of his daughter at school slid out. Carlos's face darkened as he stared at the pictures.

"I checked with the school, sir," Denis said hastily. "Your daughter is fine. I also requested them to add additional security."

Carlos wadded the vid stills of his daughter Francisca playing soccer and walking across campus, into a crumpled ball and threw them in the trash.

"Thank you, Denis," he said. "We'd better head for court now, or we'll be late."

As Carlos had expected, the jury brought in a verdict of guilty in less than 15 minutes. He invited his clerk and office staff out to celebrate with him at lunch.

Across town the verdict was received much less happily.

"You are certain we can't overturn it on appeal?" Jerome Redglove, one of the titular heads of the Red Conclave asked the man who brought the news. Redglove was a thin man with brown, sleekly groomed hair. No one looking at him would suspect him of being anything but the well-groomed, up-and-coming politician he was.

The woman he was sharing lunch with was striking. Adeline Prowd had long, silver hair, which she allowed to cascade down her back in a mermaid style coiffure. The tattoo of an eagle placed discreetly over her right eye was the only thing to mark her as the Conclave's top enforcer.

"Santana is becoming a problem," Redglove told her. "I thought you were going to take care of him."

"Since you won't let me get rid of him, I've been working under a handicap. I've been looking for a whip to tame him with, and I think I've found it. We're going to introduce his daughter to a young, ambitious captain in the Conclave. Up till now, we've only used him for a few collection and intimidation jobs, but he's anxious to move up and he's pretty enough to appeal to a fourteen-year-old."

"What's his name?"

"Jean Coudet."

Coudet had once thought becoming a member of the Red Conclave would be glamorous. After being outed about the date rape ring, he had been shunned by most of the good citizens of the colony. He received his assignment with mixed feelings. He wasn't attracted to little girls, but he told Antoni Guissipe, the Enforcer who brought him the assignment, he would do it.

"How?" Guissipe asked curiously.

Coudet had been flipping through the pages in the information Guissipe had handed him. "There is a teen hangout called the Black Dog Café she frequents. It shouldn't be hard.

Girls her age are always looking for a bad boy underdog. I'll get her to come to me."

WALKING THE LINE

OBEDIENTLY, Ava went to her room. After settling Sunrise into a comfy catamount bed, she stripped and got into the shower. It felt luxurious having a long shower; one where she didn't have to rush and save water so the next person would have enough hot water to do the same. She even used the scented soaps her mother had supplied—out in the wild she preferred the unscented variety, as some of the animals she encountered were apt to take a dislike to the scents in the soap or, which was worse, make her smell like prey.

Back in her room, she saw that the vet bot had arrived and prepared a new bottle of formula for Sunrise, who was rooting around looking for food. Still in her bathrobe, she lifted the small creature and accepted the new bottle. Sunrise latched on eagerly and preceded to stuff herself, before falling back asleep.

Ava eyed the clothes her mother had laid out. At least this time Tamara Garneys hadn't ignored her elder daughter's preference for pants, rather than a skirt. The red and white striped pants proved to be as form fitting as a skin suit, ending at the ankle where a pair of elegant, embroidered stockings slid into dainty, heeled shoes with an ornate jeweled design. The white linen blouse was a loose, off the shoulder design with a tiny puff at the shoulders, cinched in with a tight blue bustier that cupped her breasts.

She had just finished dressing when her mother's styling-bot came in, followed by Judith. It was obvious the bot had already worked her magic on the younger girl; her flaming hair was done mermaid style with pearls and tiny emeralds woven in the loose waterfall of tresses. Coupled with dramatic eye makeup to make her green eyes larger, and generous red lip dye, Judith looked eminently desirable, which the low-cut top and tight bustier emphasized.

"Please sit down, Miss Ava. I'm here to do your hair and makeup," Marie, the stylist-bot said. Resignedly, Ava sat down in the chair in front of the ornately carved dresser with its three-sided mirror in a frame matching the dresser.

Judith sprawled on Ava's bed to watch the bot work, as she used to do when she was too young to date.

"Don't mess up your hair or your dress, or Mom will have a fit," Ava warned.

"I'm being careful," her sister replied.

Ava relaxed into the sensual feel of the brush going through her hair, and the bot's nimble fingers as she wove Ava's long red curls into a mermaid wave and inserted tiny, moonstone jeweled hair pins. She kept her eyes closed when the chair was turned around to face Marie, who began applying makeup with a delicate touch no human could match.

"There, you can look now," Marie announced.

Ava stood up and looked at herself in the full-length, three-way mirror. She looked good, she was forced to admit. Her active life in the outdoors had helped to keep her figure toned. The thin vertical stripes on the pants made her legs look impossibly long, and the soft gathers of the blouse under the tight bustier gave her a fuller figure. Somehow Marie had managed to erase the tan lines on her hands and neck, blending them into the creamy white of her breast and shoulders.

"Oh, good, you're both here," Tamara said, she carried a heavy jewel box, which Marie took from her and opened to reveal an array of necklaces, bracelets and earrings. Tamara looked her daughters over thoughtfully.

"Stand up, Judith. Anyone seeing you would think you were twelve instead of an engaged woman about to be married."

Judith obediently slid off the bed. Tamara selected a gold encrusted sapphire and ruby pendant and placed it on her younger daughter's neck. She pulled out a matching pair of earrings and a bracelet before standing back. She made a twirling gesture with her finger, and Judith obediently twirled for her inspection. "Excellent," she said. "Sit down on the chair while I add the finishing touches to Ava's outfit."

"Mom, I don't need a lot of jewelry," Ava protested. "I'm not the one getting married."

"That's as may be," Tamara responded cryptically. Ava was soon decked out in an ornate pearl and moonstone necklace with matching earrings and a bracelet.

Tamara turned back to her younger daughter. "The feathered beret, I think, Marie. It will give her more height. It's a good thing Randal didn't grow up to be tall."

As she spoke, she fastened a tiny, jeweled beret with a fan of small feathers in Judith's hair.

"Let's go girls, we don't want to be late to the engagement dinner." Tamara swept both her daughters ahead of her into the parlor where their father was waiting.

"You both look lovely," he said with a proud smile.

The formal rehearsal dinner was a nightmare. The man on her right, Nicholas Bradstane, was around her age and she supposed he was thought to be good looking, but to her mind his smarmy manner did away with any advantage his looks might have given him. He was handsy too.

The disadvantage of her pants over a skirt, was there wasn't a place to hide the poniard sheath customarily strapped to her thigh under a dress, so the third time his hand tried to creep into her lap, she picked up her meat knife and holding it point down over his lap, said softly, "If you don't stop that, I'm going to change your religion."

Bradstane hastily took his hand out of her lap, and thereafter ignored her. Across the table, she looked up to meet Carlos Santana's eyes and realized he had seen the entire thing and was trying manfully not to laugh. She turned her own laugh into a cough. Carlos was their family attorney. Ava had met him earlier this year when her father and his two partners had been detained because a Red Conclave operative who worked for them was murdered in their business, Dreamedia Laboratories. There had been an instant attraction between them. She had often wondered why he had never followed up on it.

Of course, as soon as her father had been cleared, she had headed back to base camp in the Silverton Mountains the closest subsidiary mountain range of th Great Rainbow Ridge, which her team was mapping. Even if he had wanted to do anything about their mutual attraction, there hadn't been time.

Why couldn't her mother have seated Carlos next to her, instead of that prat Bradstane? At least then she would have had someone interesting to talk to. She knew why, of course; her parents figured Bradstane would be a good matrimonial candidate, but as far as Ava was concerned, their choices of men for her were still terrible.

When dinner was finally over, her mother had planned a small reception. Ava mingled with the guests as required of her, but after an hour, she slipped away to check on Sunrise.

She found the vet-bot frantically looking under furniture in her room.

"Where is she?" Ava demanded.

If it was possible for as robot to look dismayed, this one did. "She must have crawled out of the litter box and went looking for you," it said apologetically.

Just then, hearing Ava's voice, the kit staggered out from under the bed, mewling plaintively. Ava picked her up to cuddle.

"Is her bottle ready?"

"Yes." He handed it to her as well as a towel to put over her dress clothes. Ava decided to feed the kit outside. She took the outside stairs up to the top floor where the reception was taking place. At least up here, her mother couldn't accuse her of hiding from any potential suitors, but she didn't intend to draw attention to her presence out here. She sat down in a comfortable chair and arranged the towel on her lap. Sunrise, who had begun to gripe again latched onto the nipple as if she were starving.

The tranquility and quiet of the night, and the small warm body in her lap were soothing. From here, the subdued roar of voices blended with the string quartet her mother had hired into a relaxing symphony. She leaned back and closed her eyes.

After a few minutes, she realized she wasn't the only one taking advantage of the patio for privacy. Carlos Santana, the Garneys family lawyer was arguing with someone on his com. Judith had told her once she thought Carlos looked like the tall, dark and handsome Latino in all those old vids. His slender height, coupled with finely cut features and melting dark eyes certainly gave credence to the claim.

"I bet he wins over a lot of female jurors with those looks," Ava had retorted.

It didn't seem as if those attributes were winning the argument with whoever was on the other end of the com. From the tight look around his mouth, and the forced calm of his voice it was obvious he was furious. "Francisca, I said no, and I meant it. What part of no don't you understand?"

There was a brief reply, then Carlos said, "Young lady if you leave the house tonight, all hell will break over your head when I find you— Francisca! Dammit!" he said, closing the com.

He turned and spotted Ava sitting in the shadows. "I beg your pardon. I didn't see you there."

"It's alright. I take it that was your daughter?"

"Yes," he said. "I wish my wife was still alive. I don't know what to do with her. Somehow, she's gotten involved with Jean Coudet. Aside from the fact he's years too old for her (she's only fourteen) I know he's a member of the Red Conclave."

"That isn't good," Ava agreed.

"Carlos, I've been looking for you everywhere," a woman's voice announced.

Ava recognized her; it was Elinor Crawley. The other woman was a tall, cool, green-eyed blond with a slim, model's figure. They had gone to school together, and Ava had always considered her a complete bitch. If Carlos was entangled with her, he had her sympathy, although she doubted he wanted it.

"Sorry, Elinor, I wanted privacy to speak to my daughter. Shall we return to the party?"

"Did you look at that finishing school I recommended? She's just angling for attention you know. They have an excellent record for stopping these types of tantrums."

"There you are. Ava, you can't hide out here, we have guests," Tamara Garneys said, frowning.

"I was feeding Sunrise," Ava said, lifting the now sleeping catamount. "As soon as I put her back to bed, I'll be back to the party."

"Oh," Tamara said. "Don't be long dear. Your father has someone he wants you to meet."

She turned back to her guests, so she didn't see the face her daughter made, but Carlos did, and he choked back a laugh. Ava stuck out her tongue at him.

CLOSE TO MIDNIGHT

IT WAS RAINING when Ava woke the next morning. Not an unusual circumstance as the area around the capital city of Savona got doused in water every other day. Upon her return from the bathroom, the vet-bot handed her Sunrise and a warmed bottle of Catamount formula, which the small creature sucked dry and whined for more.

"I think she's ready for a little solid food, Miss Ava." The vet-bot said.

"It sure looks like it," Ava agreed. "What kind did Dr. Peele recommend?"

48

The bot pulled a small packet labeled 'kitten starter' out of its pouch and squeezed it into a small dish which it sat on the floor. "She's apt to be messy," he said, taking Sunrise from her and setting her down in front of the dish. He put a little on a finger and showed it to the kit before letting her lick it off. Sunrise dove eagerly into the food dish, smearing the food liberally over her nose and paws when she put both front feet into the dish.

The bot was cleaning Sunrise's face and paws while Ava dressed. After a moment's thought, she strapped a poniard sheath to her thigh, checking the sharpness of the blade before sliding it into the leather sheath.

"I brought you something," Judith announced as she bounced into the

49

room. She held out a soft-sided purse with a long crossbody strap. "I used this when Licorice was smaller. Sunrise can ride in the front pocket, and you can slip a bottle and maybe a food packet in the rear. It's insulated."

Ava accepted it gingerly before showing it to Sunrise, who, after sniffing it thoroughly, crawled inside the fur lined front pouch. "She likes it," Ava exclaimed in surprise.

Judith nodded. "It probably smells like mother's milk. I had it cleaned, but smells linger. I came in here to invite you to come with Randal and me to the Portal Opening this morning. Tash and Devon will be coming through. It will also save you from whatever social function Mom has planned."

"Yes, I'd love to. I'm sure she has plans to attend some social thing where she thinks I'll meet Mr. Right. *Anything* is better than that!"

Judith giggled. "I saw that guy trying to grope you at dinner. It would have been funnier if you'd really stabbed him though."

Ava laughed. "What time does the Portal open?"

"Just before lunch time. I'm planning on showing them my new house too. Want to come?"

Ava grinned at her. "The longer I get to stay out of Mom's match-making clutches, the better."

Judith snorted. Since she and Randal had been affianced when they were children, she had never come under the type of pressure to choose a husband Ava had. Ava was a fourth-generation colonist. She knew what was expected of her. Sooner or later, she would need to marry to fulfil her duty to the colony. As was traditional in the Renaissance, parents usually chose their children's life partners. The young couples involved *did* have the option of refusing a proposed match, which meant parents put single children under a lot of pressure to present an attractive prospect to future partners. The trouble was she and her parents didn't agree on what was a good match for her, and Ava intensely disliked being put on display for future husbands. One of the reasons she had chosen a career that kept her out of most of the social whirl except for holidays or occasions like her sister's wedding.

Randal picked the two girls up in front of their house. He greeted Judith with a kiss, which she returned with enthusiasm. As her mother had mentioned, Randal wasn't overly tall for a man, but the tight breeches showed off his muscled legs, and he moved with the effortless ease of a master swordsman, which he was.

"I was just thinking how well you and Judith look together," Ava said as he helped her into the carriage.

"I'm a lucky guy," he agreed. "I'm looking forward to seeing Devon again. And Tash too, of course."

The robot driver parked their sled (which resembled an old-fashioned carriage) just outside the staging area, while the two girls waited for the Portal to open.

Barsoom's portal to Laughing Mountain had come out near the equator in the tropic zone. Rather than move the Portal to a more temperate climate, the original founders had decided not to waste resources by moving it. The structure had a gently sloping roof supported by steel pillars and was open to the air. Since it rained every other day, the floor was covered with rough cobblestones to minimize slippage.

The colony founders hadn't made much effort to clear the area around the portal, except for allowing space to park transports dropping off or picking up people and items the colony couldn't manufacture themselves, so the Portal site was surrounded by lush vegetation.

Like most things in the colony, the transports were not what they seemed. Incoming supplies were pulled through the colorful portal with golf carts attached to wagons. Robots in the colorful government uniforms would unload the wagons drawn by the carts and re-load them into the Modern transports disguised as old-fashioned horse drawn wagons. Of course, the horses too were robotic and mainly for show; the transports were powered by Gregor crystals imported from Lemuria.

"There they are!" Randal said, waving at a couple riding behind the driver on a golf cart. He took off for the cart and swung into the passenger seat. "We're over there," he directed the driver, one of Mark Connor's sons towards the parked carriage.

Judith gave Tash a welcoming hug. "Tash, you remember my sister Ava, don't you?"

"Yes, I do," Tash replied, shaking hands. She was about medium height for a woman, with finely drawn features, blue-black hair, just now pulled back into a ponytail and a lush figure. She had a crossbody soft-sided animal pouch slung across her body. A lavender hued catamount popped her head out, spied Licorice and struggled to climb out of the purse. "Take it easy Fidget," Tash said. "Give me a minute to fasten your leash."

"You have a catamount," Ava said in surprise. "What if Earth-Gov police spot her?"

"I just tell everyone she's a new variety of hairless cat," Tash said.

She looked with interest at Ava's pouch when Sunrise woke up and poked her head out. "I see you have a pet with you as well. What is it?"

Ava chuckled. "This is Sunrise. She is a Catamount, but she's a different variety than you two have. Her variety are called Hairy Catamounts. I rescued her from a pack of Kevlars just as her mom died."

"Kevlars? What are they?" Tash asked eagerly. "I'm trying to assemble a photo diary of the various animals found on each colony. Of course it can't be published on Earth, but there's no reason why it can't be sold on the colonies."

"Kevlars are a carnivore found in the higher elevations, like the Hairy Catamounts," Ava told her. "They occupy the same evolutionary niche as wolves did on earth. The scientist's think they are genetically related somewhere way back."

"If we have time, I'd love for you to take me to where you saw them. I'd pay you, of course."

Judith laughed. "She'd probably do it for free if it kept her out of Mom's clutches. She and my dad are vested in putting her on the Marriage Mart while she's here."

Ava made a face at her sister, but agreed, "She's right. I hate that stuff."

Tash frowned at her. "Your parents didn't seem like the type to force you into anything. I've met them remember."

"They aren't," Ava replied, "They won't force me to accept anyone, but they are insistent I parade myself before all the eligible men while I'm here, and I hate being put on display."

"I would too," Tash sympathized.

Randal and Devon had finished loading the luggage and Devon's equipment into the luggage area atop the carriage and in the boot in the rear.

"Did anyone tell you that Carter Willis arranged our own house for us?" Devon asked Tash as he and Randal settled into the coach.

"Oh, wow," Judith said. "Are you going to accept?"

"Sure, why not?" Devon replied. "I understand it comes fully furnished with its own robot crew. That will make it a lot easier than asking Randal's parents to host us."

"Not that they wouldn't be delighted to do so," Randal said, "But the house is currently full of visiting relatives here for the wedding."

"I'll have to write and thank him," Tash said.

"I'm so glad to have you to do that stuff," Devon told her. "I'd probably forget to do it, if I thought of it in the first place."

Tash laughed, kissing him on the cheek. "Yes, I know. When do we get to see it?"

"We'll drop your stuff off there first, before we go on to our new house. We're planning on having a picnic lunch there."

The house Willis had rented for Devon and Tash was on the smaller size as far as Barsoomian houses went. It was only two stories, with the bedrooms on the second floor and rooms for dining, cooking and relaxing on the first. It floated on the edge of the Grantois Lake, its plasticrete foundation supported by steel coated pillars sunk deep into the lake. Like most houses on or near the edge of the lake, it could be lifted to keep the waters from flooding it whenever the lake rose due to the heavy rains. The home was surrounded by a plasticrete dock, allowing visitors to disembark before walking up the steps leading onto the wrap-around porch on the first floor.

As soon as their sled landed on the dock, two liveried robots began unloading the luggage and Devon's equipment. Randal handed Devon a set of key cards, one of which he gave to Tash.

"Let's go inside," Tash said, "I'm eager to see what it looks like."

Laughing, Devon offered her his arm to escort her into the foyer, where another robot servant waited to take their hats.

MIDNIGHT FRENZY

THE PARTY that night was a gala affair. Tamara had again yielded to Ava's preference for pants, rather than a dress to wear to the ball. She had sent her styling bot to ensure both her daughters looked their best. However, when Ava and Judith entered their common room, Tamara's eyes riveted on the poniard strapped to her elder daughters thigh.

"You can't go to a party wearing that thing!" she exclaimed, pointing at the slim dagger. "Go and take it off at once!"

"Why?" Ava said stubbornly. "You are wearing one. So is Judith. Mine is just out in the open."

"But—Agustin, say something!" Tamara turned to her husband.

"What would you like me to say?" her husband inquired. "She's right."

"But it's so off-putting to potential suitors," Tamara complained.

"If they are put off by what I'm wearing, so be it," Ava declared. "They need to know who I am the sooner the better."

"That's true," her father agreed.

Her mother rolled her eyes but dropped the subject. "Well, let's get going then. We don't want to be late,"

Randal had swung by to pick up Tash and Devon. Once through the receiving line, he looked around eagerly for his fiancé, his eyes lighting up when he spotted Judith.

"You look beautiful," he told her.

"Thank you," she said with a smile, returning the kiss.

"I see you brought party clothes with you," she told Tash.

Tash grinned. "Laughing Mountains seamstress shop was very accommodating, when I showed her the dress your mother gave me, and the clothes Devon borrowed from Randal. I also got Mark to give me a few lessons on how to handle a knife," Tash said with a giggle.

"I'm glad," Judith said. "Aunt Carmen over-ruled Dad and insisted Ava and I learn the rudiments—according to her, everyone should know how to handle a weapon."

"Mark thought I was cracked too, but when I explained that everyone here carried one, he agreed I should learn enough not to cut myself."

After the briefest of greetings, Tamara had drawn Ava away to introduce her to some of the eligible bachelors attending the party.

Ava was polite to them, but she was relieved when none of them asked for a second dance. Which might have been due to her openly carrying a weapon or to her obvious disinterest in them personally.

After the final partner had left her at the edge of the dance floor, she slipped outside, allowing the evening breeze to cool her cheeks.

"Sorry, I didn't realize someone else was out here—Oh, it's you," she finished when Carlos turned around.

Even in the dark she could feel the tension rolling off him in waves. "Is something wrong?"

"Francisca's gone," he said.

"Gone as in disappeared? Did she run away?"

"I assume so. None of her friends have seen or heard from her—or so they claim."

"Do you think they are lying?"

"It's going to sound crazy, but I hope they are. Because if they aren't lying, it means she might have run to that bastard Coudet."

"I'm not familiar with that name. Who is he?"

"Aside from being years too old for her, he is probably a member of the Red Conclave. Your brother-in-law's friend Devon fought a duel with him when he was here last time."

"I hadn't heard about that. Why did Devon fight him?"

"Apparently, he and some of his friends gave Tash a date rape drug at a party. The rumor goes, they intended to gang rape her. She wouldn't have been the first either."

"Have you checked the hospital?"

"Yes. They haven't seen her."

"What did Coudet say when you asked him if he'd seen your daughter?"

"I can't find the bastard. I came here tonight so I could speak to Randal about where he found him last time. Is he here yet?"

"Yes, he was waiting for Judith when we got here. C'mon, let's go find him."

They ran Randal and Devon to earth in an alcove near the punch bowl along with the group he and Judith hung out with, consisting of Ailwin Doreward, Oliver Coffyn, and Jocelyn Dering who was engaged to Ailwin.

"What's the matter sis?" Judith asked, seeing Ava had her serious face on.

"Carlos needs to find Jean Coudet," Ava announced.

"What do you want with that creep?" Judith asked Carlos.

"My fourteen-year-old daughter ran away from home yesterday. I want to ask him if he's seen her."

"He's bad news," Ailwin said, giving his fiancé a reassuring hug. He and Jocelyn made an odd pair: he was tall and lanky, and she was short and full figured.

"How did he get acquainted with your daughter?" Judith asked Carlos. "After we outed him to the families about the date rape drugs, everyone quit asking him to any kind of social gathering."

"I don't know how she met him. Somewhere she got the idea he was wrongfully accused of that crime. We've been arguing about it for weeks," Carlos said ruefully.

"I've sort of kept an eye on him since you've been gone," Randal told Devon thoughtfully. "Let me make some coms. I have a few friends who just might know where he is."

"He runs with a pack," Oliver said, a frown on his dark-skinned face. "Why don't we all go with you to confront him?"

"Is it dangerous?" Jocelyn asked anxiously.

"We won't go looking for him unarmed." Her fiancé told her.

Carlos had been watching who Randal had commed. Randal had invoked a cone of silence, so he couldn't hear what was said, but he recognized the man on the other end of the com; it was Andri Gavreau. Officially Gavreau was retired, but unofficially he was suspected of being member of the Black Templars. For Randal to com him so casually, he must be a member as well.

"Thank you, sir." Randal concluded the conversation and snapped off the com before turning back to the group.

"Well?" Carlos asked.

"It seems Coudet has moved up in the world since the last time we dealt with him," he said to Devon.

Devon nodded. "Not surprising since we took down Albion's little kidnapping ring. They would have had spaces to fill."

"Did Gavreau say anything about my daughter?" Carlos asked.

"Not her specifically. However, Coudet seems to have been promoted to handling security for the Prostitution arm of the Red Conclave."

"Prostitution?" Carlos felt sick. It must have shown on his face, because Ava laid a comforting hand on his arm.

"How old is your daughter?" Randal asked.

"Francisca is only fourteen," Carlos replied, swallowing his gorge.

Randal looked thoughtfully at him. "Finding her won't be easy. By the time we do she might not be the innocent she was when she disappeared," he warned.

"It doesn't matter. She's my little girl, dammit. Did you find out where this Coudet hangs out?"

"Gavreau gave me the name of a few places. He also instructed me to go with you when you start searching."

Ava heard her sister draw a quick breath of protest.

"I'm sorry, Darling," Randal told her. "I need to do this."

Judith swallowed. "Alright, but I need to know where you intend to look." Randal frowned at her. "It's too dangerous."

"Then you better make sure *you* don't disappear, you hear me?"

"I hear you," he said, a note of resignation in his voice. "I'll com you before we enter each destination."

Judith nodded. "You'd better."

"We're going to need more weapons than we are carrying," Devon said practically.

THE MAN IN THE IRON MASK

ANDRI GAVREAU, was indeed a member of the Black Templars governing board. He closed his com and turned to his companions. "You heard?"

"Yes," Guillaume Peele, a tall, slim man with greying hair, practically rubbed his hands together in glee. "Maybe this time we have a whip to tame Coudet."

"Maybe," Thomasine Villars who was in her sixties but still beautiful, said pessimistically. "It won't be the first time we thought we had him, and he slipped out of the noose."

Joan Merton, the youngest of the board members was in her late thirties. "I don't like the sound of this teenage girl. If he's passed her on to some of his associates, she could be in bad shape by the time Langston and the others find her."

"You heard her father—he doesn't care what they've done to her. she's still his little girl."

"Ummn, what do we know about this Carlos Santana?" asked Guillaume Peele. He was Randal Langston's boss in the Templars.

"He's a lawyer," answered Mathieu Heroux. "I believe he represented a couple of actors in that contract negotiation scandal a few years back. He's also the family attorney for the Garney's."

"Isn't Agustin Garneys one of our operatives? He and his partners own Dreamedia Laboratories, the business we asked to employ Simone Gusset before she was murdered." Joan supplied.

"Santana's a cool customer in court," Mathieu said. "I don't know how he'll react when it's about his family. I think we'd better keep an eye of the search party." Villars said.

"I agree with Thomasine," said Peele, "Devon Morton is back for Langston's wedding. He and Coudet have a history."

Gavreau frowned, "Just how much of a hothead is this Morton?"

"He doesn't look it, but he's a tough customer," Peele stated. "Last time he was here, Langston asked that he be given honorary Templar membership. Together, he and Randal Langston made a good team."

"Where did you tell them to look for Coudet?" Heroux asked.

Gavreau shrugged. "Coudet's moved up in the world. He hangs out at that new place on Government row now."

"The Violet Glass Pub?" inquired Peele. "Are they grooming him for a political office?"

"Not after that debacle with the date rape drugs," Heroux snorted. "More likely he's supposed to be gathering information the Red Conclave can use to pressure a few politicos."

"Well now, Perhaps I'll drop in for lunch one of these days," Peele said. "It could prove interesting. Especially if Langston and Morton come in looking for Coudet."

"Getting a little tired of retirement?" Villars asked with a grin.

"Not at all. Not at all. I just like to enjoy a good meal with a few friends."

NIGHT HUNTER

CARLOS STOOD outside the trendy Pub with Randal, Devon and the two men who had served as Devon's seconds in the duel with Coudet. Coudet's new hangout was a step up from the Green Dragon. From outside the Violet Glass looked inviting, everything a renaissance pub ought to be. Stacked boulders and soft wooden tree trunks sat on the floating slab. Nearby was a parking structure for the customer's sleds and carriages. The darkened glass in the windows made seeing into the pub difficult although they created a warm inviting glow.

"Is he in there?" Carlos asked. The urge to charge inside, find Coudet and shake him like a rat until he disgorged Francisca's whereabouts grew stronger every moment.

Randal cast a wary eye at him. "Take it easy, Santana. Wait for Ailwin to come out. He and Oliver went in to ask for him."

"Would they tell them the truth?" Carlos demanded.

"Oh, I think so," Randal said calmly. "What information Ailwin doesn't get by outsmarting them, Oliver will charm out of them."

Carlos eyed the two young men with him thoughtfully. "This isn't the first time you two hunted for Coudet, is it?"

"Nope," Devon agreed. "He's got a bad rep for messing with women and girls—"

"Uh Oh, here comes security," Randal said.

Security was a tall, muscled individual, with the confident air of a man who can handle trouble. "Are you gentlemen lost?" he asked, his hand resting on his hip near his pistol. The firearm might have looked like an old-fashioned flintlock, but Carlos knew it wasn't. Security was authorized to carry pulse pistols. On Barsoom they just looked like a flintlock firearm.

Randal opened his mouth, but Carlos got there first. "Actually, we're searching for my daughter. She's fourteen but looks older. She has dark hair and eyes. You haven't seen anyone who looks like that have you?"

The security guard frowned in concern. "Was she alone?"

"Well, she might have been, but she might also have accompanied Jean

Coudet. I know she was fascinated by him, but he's far too old for her."

The guard had a daughter of his own. "I understand," he said. "I dread the day my daughter gets old enough to date. I haven't seen her myself. Do you want me to ask around?"

"Please. You can reach me at this com number." Carlos pulled out a card case and extracted a business card from it.

The guard took it.

"Thank you, officer--"

"Georges Vanderlin, If I see your daughter, I'll be sure and call you, Mr. Santana."

By this time Oliver and Ailwin had exited the pub. Randal waited until the security guard was out of earshot before he asked, "Was Coudet in there?"

"Not on the main floor," Ailwin said. "But he might have been in the snug. We didn't manage to get inside that."

"If you got in and found Coudet, you might not have gotten out," Randal said dryly.

"I'll have you know—" Oliver began.

"Never mind that," Carlos said irritably. "Does this place have a back door?"

"Oh, yeah, with a 180-decibel alarm!" Ailwin snorted. "No, our best bet is to wait for him to come out and grab him then."

"If we follow him home, we can grab him easier," Devon said. "Well, he has to sleep somewhere, doesn't he?"

Carlos waited alone outside the Violet Pub for Coudet to exit and head home for the night. It was cloudy and the two moons that had been the reason for settling the colony here were obscured by the cloud cover, as so often happened in these lower elevations. Ha had persuaded his younger posse to go back to the party and pay attention to their ladies.

"I don't have anyone waiting for me to return," he told them.

"I'll see if I can turn up a home address for him from my contacts," Randal said.

"Thank you," Carlos told him.

He wasn't afraid of being spotted because the sleek, black, two-man cruiser blended into the night sky. Like many airsleds on Barsoom, the one owned by Carlos resembled a bird; the control seats were in the hooked nose cone, and the sides had been shaped like folded bird wings. The tail held cargo space as well as flight stabilizer controls. Earlier in his career, when he had toyed with the idea of permanently becoming a bounty hunter, he outfitted the cruiser with stealth. The outer covering was of Matte Black paint covered armor from Arcadia. He had owned the cruiser a long time. Francesca had never seen it. She thought her father was an old fuddy-duddy and he hadn't tried to convince her otherwise.

He had been a wild young man before he met Francisca's mother Gillian. He had been accounted a deadly duelist; Accomplished with either a sword or a pistol, he seldom met his equal on the dueling field. Gillian had changed all that, and when Francisca came along a few months later, it had cemented his change to responsible citizen.

Gillian's death and the child she carried in a sled accident had left him rootless with the responsibility of rearing their child as a single parent. He now felt he had failed her. Part of his rage at Coudet was due to that feeling of failure. Letting the rage ride him hard, he sat in his vehicle, waiting for his prey to appear. No consideration of civilized behavior was going to stop him finding his daughter. He wouldn't fail her a second time. Coudet would tell him where he was keeping her or where he had sent her.

Carlos had sent the young men away principally because what he planned to do to make Coudet talk wasn't going to be civilized.

When Coudet finally came out of the pub, he was accompanied by two others. Filippo Brunelleschi and Giulio Lupin. This was no surprise as the pair now accompanied him most places. Francisca was not with them.

The house Coudet was heading for was out of town. Carlos liked that because it meant what he was about to do was less likely to draw attention from the police. He waited until their sled was settling down on the dock to disgorge its passengers before he fired a pulse blast at it. He aimed at the underside edge of the sled so that it over balanced and tipped on its side, trapping its passengers. In case anyone in the house was considering coming out to rescue them, he also fired a shot at the door of the house. Leaving his own sled in hover mode, he stepped out onto the side of the wrecked sled and cut a hole in the door with a laser torch. All three of the men inside were bruised and shaken. Coudet had been driving so he was closest to the front of the sled. Carlos shot the other two to ensure they couldn't try to help Coudet when he reached down into the sled and seized Coudet by the collar, dragging him up and outside. He flopped the still dazed Coudet onto his belly and secured the man's hands behind him with tie straps. He dragged Coudet's dead weight into his own sled. He threw him in the cargo space, and took off with his prisoner, not noticing the dark sled watching him from around the curve of the lake.

Before he married Gillian and settled down, Carlos had maintained a hideout of sorts in a cave up above the city. He hadn't visited there in quite a while, so he was prepared for the place to be a mess. It was obvious when he landed the sled inside, that an animal had been using it as a den. There were old bones chewed by teeth around the entrance.

The animal hadn't been able to get into the man-sized cage in the back of the cave. Since his planned career as a bounty hunter had meant he might need a secure place to keep captives, he spent a little time and money adding sanitary facilities to the cage; he had no desire to clean up after his captured outlaws if they needed to use the bathroom.

There was castoff debris where something had made a nest. Carlos used a blower to blow most of the debris out of the cave. The blower he used sounded like the growling of a huge animal. When Carlos re-entered the sled, he found a wide-eyed Coudet braced up against the wall. "What was that?" The man asked.

Carlos grinned at him. "If you cooperate, maybe I won't let you make its acquaintance."

He sat down in the chair facing the cargo space and took out his knife, picking up a piece of wood to whittle on. The knife was long and thin with a sharp point it wasn't really made to Whittle wood, but he was betting Coudet was too rattled to pay attention to that.

"What do you want to know?" Coudet asked, vainly trying to keep his voice from wavering.

"Where is my daughter Coudet?" Carlos asked.

Coudet eyed him. "Your daughter? What is her name?" He asked regaining a measure of confidence since he was now sure Carlos didn't intend to kill him out of hand.

Carlos leaned forward, allowing the sharp point of the knife to touch Coudet's cheek. If he held perfectly still, the knife wouldn't cut the skin; but if he moved even a millimeter, he was going to get cut. "My ancestors on earth were priests and members of the Inquisition. We captured religious fanatics of course, but we also interrogated prisoners for royalty. One of the things the family diaries describe is

how to skin a man. You start by just
making a shallow cut and then peeling
a little bit of skin back a small
piece at a time. I hear it's
exquisitely painful. Shall we find
out?"

Coudet's eyes rolled back in his
head, and he fainted. Carlos looked
at him in disgust.

"Looks like you overshot the mark
with that one. I think he fainted,"
Randal Langston observed.

Carlos jumped and whirled around.
He had been so concentrated on
Coudet, he hadn't noticed Randal and
Devon landing until they came into
the sled. "How the Hell did you find
me?"

"I tagged your sled with one of
these, and we followed you," Devon
replied. He held up a small, flat
disc. "That was pretty good work on

Coudet's sled with the plasma blaster."

"That spiel about the Inquisition was good too. It sure scared the shit out Coudet." Randal added.

"Yeah," Devon said. "Maybe we should have brought along some of those adult diapers. If he's messed in his pants, it's going to stink."

"Is that what that smell is?"

"He's awake," Devon said.

Coudet glared at them, water dripping off the end of His nose from the small amount Carlos had thrown at him to bring him out of his faint. At that moment, Coudet hated Carlos for making him look weak and Devon and Randal for being witness to his weakness. "Francisca was sent out to Sivano to be trained. She'll be a good little whore by the time he done with her— "

Carlos backhanded him across the face, bloodying his lip. "Where?"

"Will you let me go if I tell you?"

"I'll let you go when I have my daughter back safe."

"Sivano has a house out by the Rosewood Plantation Settlement. She's probably still there. It usually takes him about 3 weeks to train a whore into proper obedience."

They left Coudet shut up in the cage and returned to the party, which despite the late hour was still going on.

Coudet did a lot of yelling in protest at being caged up.

"We should go back to the party," Carlos said, "we don't want anyone to connect us to his disappearance. It might make it harder to find Francisca."

"Can he get out?" Randal asked.

"I doubt it," Carlos replied. "That padlock can only be opened by someone with my DNA. I'll meet you back at the party."

THE COLD HAND OF DARKNESS

JUDITH THREW her arms around Randal's neck when he returned. He returned the kiss with enthusiasm.

"Wow," Devon said, "Don't I get one of those?" he asked Tash.

She laughed and kissed him. "Now tell us what happened,"

"Did you find her?" Ava had managed to slip away from her mother and make her way back to where Judith and Tash were waiting for their men to return.

"Yes, did you find her?" Tash asked as well.

"No, but we think we have a location where they're keeping her," Devon said. "Have you ever heard of a plantation named Rosewoods?"

Judith shook her head. "No."

Randal frowned. "I haven't either. What we need is a map."

"You will be able to find the Plantation on a map, but I doubt you will be able to find where they are keeping Francisca on it," Ava interjected. "The place is huge and there are probably several dozen sheds where they might be keeping her for training. The one you want is disguised; it isn't really a shed. It's a building with a basement. The girls being trained are kept down there. I was only out there once, but I think I can find the right shed again."

Carlos looked at her in surprise. "When were you out there?"

"A friend of mine was kidnapped. The kidnappers hid her out there. If they were caught, they planned to use her location to bargain for their freedom."

"I remember something about that," Judith exclaimed. "You remember, Randal. The Consigliere kidnapping."

"Yes, I do remember that. We were about twelve when it happened. But how did you come to be on the search team Ava?"

She shrugged. "I eavesdropped on one of the gangs who were a part of the kidnapping ring. I told Dad, but he had such a fit about me being anywhere near them, I was afraid he wouldn't do anything about it. So, I snuck out of the house and went out to the area they had mentioned. The place is so big—I don't think you could find the right shed even with directions. I'll have to go with you."

"Mom will have a fit if she finds out," Judith warned her.

"I know," Ava nodded. "You'll have to run interference for me."

Judith made a face. "Why am I always the one who gets left behind to wait?"

"Just lucky, I guess. If we leave about 4 AM the sun should be coming up by the time we reach the plantation."

Carlos pulled a watch fob out of his vest pocket. "That's about an hour and a half from now. Where do you want to meet?"

"My new house," Randal said. "It's far enough out of town so we shouldn't attract notice."

Carlos looked at Ava. "Where do you want me to pick you up?"

"You aren't," she said. "I'll be taking my sled. I will be less likely to set off any alarms when I investigate the shed to make sure she's there. If she is, I'll com you, okay?"

"No. It's too dangerous," he said. "Agustin would never forgive me if I let his daughter run into danger that way—"

"Carlos, a good attorney should know when you've lost an argument, and you've lost this one. I'm going and I am riding my own sled."

She turned to Judith and Tash, aware of Carlos glaring holes in her back. "Will you watch Sunrise for me?"

"Sure," Tash said. "Is she still taking a bottle?"

"Yes, but I'm starting her on solid food. She's kind of a messy eater, I'm afraid."

Ava wasn't happy to find Judith waiting for her in the sled garage when she crept out of the house later that morning.

"What are you doing here?" she demanded. "You're supposed to be watching Sunrise and distracting Mom today."

Judith grinned at her. "Don't worry about Mom—I sicced Aunt Carmen on her. She'll be lucky if she has time to breathe today. And Tash is going to come by and pick up Licorice, Sunrise and the vet bot and take them back to her place."

"How did you rope Aunt Carmen into this?" Ava demanded. "She must be eighty if she's a day."

"She is. She also used to be pretty wild when she was younger. She was delighted to join into another 'adventure'."

More seriously, Ava said, "This isn't going to be a thrill ride, little sister."

Judith shook a finger at her. "Oh, no you don't, Big Sister. You need backup on this jaunt, and you know it. I can shoot and fence as well as you can. You might as well learn when you've lost the argument too. I'm going."

"Dammit," Ava said. "What kind of weapons did you bring?"

"I raided Randal's weapons closet. I have a long-range pulse rifle, a pistol, a sleeve dagger (I brought one of those for you too), a second dagger in my boot, and a rapier. Good enough?"

Ava looked at her sister, stunned. "Where are you hiding them? All I see are the rapier and the rifle."

"Body Armor from Arcadia. Tash got it for me. I have some for you as well; it belongs to Tash but she's about your size and she isn't going to need it since she's on catamount duty."

She tossed a package at her sister, who caught it. "Thanks, I left mine back at base camp." Ava stripped and pulled on the shirt and pants which fitted itself to her body. "Wow! This is better stuff than mine. I'll have to order some when we get back."

She mounted her sled and pulled on her helmet, turning on the night vision. Judith copied her. They set off quietly, unaware that Randal and Devon were watching them.

"You were right, dammit," Randal said. "I wonder why Tash isn't with them as well?"

Devon sighed. "I got lucky. Judith talked her into staying behind to keep an eye on the catamounts."

"Time to go hunting," Randal said, kicking his sled into gear. They set off after the two girls who were running without lights so as not to attract attention.

Carlos followed them in his black sled.

Although Savano was near a lake, Ava headed out into the country. The area surrounding the city was surrounded by a continuous, closed canopy of large tree leaves. Broken in places by tall trees reaching enormous heights whose tops poked up out of the top layer. The foliage forced the sled posse to travel slowly because it was necessary to dodge between trees inhabited with all kinds of birds, lizards and animals whose feet never touched the forest floor. To Judith's disgust it was also full of insects. She was thankful for the body armor and helmet she wore as it protected her from the attacking insects. Most of Barsoom's personal conveyances were also reminiscent of birds. However, the one-man airsleds came equipped with a saddle for riding, handlebars for control, and a large clear windshield in case the rider preferred not to waste power by enabling the protective shield bubble. Since Ava hadn't turned hers on, Judith hadn't either.

Ava finally reached the edge of a cultivated field just as the sun was coming up. The field was empty except for the robots who were cutting back the native plants to prevent them from choking out the imported plants under cultivation.

Ava led them over to a tool shed which serviced the robots and set down behind it. Judith followed her.

"What now?" she asked.

Her sister raised the faceplate on her helmet. "I'm waiting for our tag-a-longs to come out of the forest."

"We were followed? By whom?"

"I'm pretty sure one of them was Carlos. That big black sled he's driving wasn't meant to weave in and out through the forest the way we were. And I'm guessing the other two sleds are driven by Randal and Devon Morton."

The two falcon shaped sleds ridden by Randal and Devon were the first to poke their noses out of the forest. They hovered just outside the cultivated area until a larger black looking bird of prey slid out. Ava tapped her com.

"Over here, behind the shed," she sent.

She and Judith waited until the three sleds had joined them.

"Is this the right shed?" Carlos asked. His sled was enclosed, so he opened the door and steped out.

"No," Ava said, keeping her voice low.

"Can those robots hear us?" Randal asked. He too spoke softly.

"I doubt it," Ava said. "They're programmed to hear noises at a certain volume because their programming includes keeping large predators and deer out of the crop fields." She eyed the three men. "What did you plan to do when you got here?"

"Split up and search the sheds for the one where Francisca is being kept," Carlos answered.

"That will work," Ava said. "I downloaded this this morning. I doubt if Francisca is being held at one of the official sheds, but we need to check them anyway." She sent them a farm blueprint of all the buildings on the plantation.

"Which one are you taking first?" Devon asked.

"I've got the co-ordinates of the one my friend was held in," she replied. "I'll go there first; on the off chance they are still using it."

"You think they moved operations to a different site because that one was discovered?"

"Maybe. It's what I would have done."

"Wait," Devon said. "Everyone hold out your wrist com; I have a download that may make our search easier. I'm sending you a program to scan for life signs. Just point your com at the building and it will flash green if it senses human life."

EVIL IS AS EVIL DOES

AVA LED off into the trees again. She and Judith stopped at the edge of what had once be a clearing. Although the shed looked abandoned and neglected, Ava didn't believe it had been empty since she had rescued Darlene from it ten years ago. The foliage surrounding it had been recently cut back.

She said as much to Judith.

"My controller doesn't show any life signs," Judith protested.

"That just means there is no one in the top section," Ava replied. "The basement is shielded from scans.

I will have to go inside to confirm it's abandoned."

"Don't you mean we will have to go inside?"

"No, I need you to stay out here and make sure Sivano doesn't send anyone to check things out if I set off an alarm."

"Oh, I see. That makes sense, I guess."

Ava took a portable code cracker out of the sled's saddlebags and hooked it on her belt."

"Where did you get that?" Judith asked.

Ava grinned at her. "It's left over from my misspent youth. I opened my hidey-hole after we got back from the party. This little toy is something I used to take with me when I was a teenager."

"How come I never heard about any of this stuff?" Judith demanded.

"Mom and Dad were trying to keep how wild I was under wraps so I wouldn't ruin my chance of a good marriage."

Judith dismounted and unlimbered her pulse rifle as she watched her sister's

Figure 1Ava about to enter the shack to rescue Francisca & Tommasa

cat-footed progress toward the shed's door which was standing ajar. When Ava slipped inside, she checked the loads on the gun, cranking the pulse charges up to maximum. She had no issues with killing whoever came to check out the alarm.

It was dark in the shed. Ava touched her helmet controls, re-instating the low light filter on the faceplate.

The door to the basement was just as she remembered it. She set the code cracker beside the keypad and turned it on. The cracker turned a dim red while it worked. It took longer than she remembered. Well, it was old, she probably needed to download and upgrade to the newest program. Finally, after a long, stretch of time, it flashed green, and the lock clicked as the door opened.

Quietly, she crept down the stairs. Her com showed two life signs, both females.

She stepped out of the stairway and slid sideways so her back was to the wall. She didn't see any active robots, so she approached the two girls chained to the wall. Both girls were sitting on the floor. Their wrist chains were too short to sit comfortably, and their arms were stretched tightly upward. The chains on their ankles were also too short to sit easily, so both girls had their legs curled at an awkward angle. They were dressed in Tee-shirts and panties. Neither one was wearing a bra.

"Francisca?" she asked, and the dark-haired girl lookup at her, but she didn't speak. Close up she also smelled faintly of vomit. She must have barfed up the drug they had given her.

"Who's your friend?" Ava asked.

The other girl lifted her head. "My name is Tommasa de'Rossi, her name is Francisca Santana. Are you here to free us?"

"Yes, I am." Ava replied. "You're remarkably coherent for someone who's been given the obedience drugs." As she spoke, she set the code cracker next to Francisca's wrist shackle. When it opened, her arm dropped limply to her lap and Ava moved on to the other one.

"That's because I seem to have a natural resistance to their filthy drugs," Tommasa said. "She threw hers up." She added, gesturing with her chin to Francisca. "Some girls do that. I think she may be allergic to it—they had to give her oxygen after she barfed."

"Hummn," Ava finished unlocking Francisca's ankles and moved on to Tommasa. "How soon will they be back?"

"I'm not sure," the girl replied. "There's no clocks in here and it's hard to tell how much time is elapsing."

"Okay," Ava told her. "Stand up to make sure you have circulation back in your legs."

She pulled Francisca to her feet and the girl stood swaying there. Grimly, Ava knelt and pulled her over a shoulder in a fireman's carry.

"Follow me," she told Tommasa.

When they came out of the basement, Ava heard the unmistakable sound of Judith's rifle being fired.

Ava tapped her com. "Judith? Is it safe to come out?"

"Yes, but hurry. He was alone but he might have gotten off a signal before I took him out."

Ava drew her pistol and went to the door. "C'mon Tommasa," she said. "We're going to move fast. Can you run?"

"Yes. If you have another pistol, I know how to fire one."

Ava stepped over the fallen guard. She could smell the scorched flesh and plastic he was giving off. Apparently, her little sister had no compunctions in shooting to kill.

"Take his—he won't be needing it," she said.

Tommasa stooped and pulled the guards pistol and holster off his body, grimacing at the reek of the burnt man. She buckled it on as she ran.

"Did you com the others?" Ava asked.

"Yes, and I sent them the coordinates of this place. They should be here soon." Judith eyed Tommasa, "Who is this?"

Tommasa straightened her body. "My name is Tommasa de'Rossi. Thank you for rescuing me."

"You're Welcome," Judith told her. "Climb on behind me; we aren't out of the woods yet."

Ava groaned. "That is the most terrible pun—" she began just as two silver, falcon shaped sleds popped out of the forest.

"You got her!" Randal exclaimed.

"What's the matter with her?" Devon asked.

Ava had managed to get Francisca mounted on her sled, but she was having to hold the girl steady with one hand.

"It's probably the drugs they give their 'trainees'," she told him. "We need to get both these girls checked out by a doctor as soon as possible."

Carlos's big black sled finally pushed its way into the clearing. He set it down and got out.

"Francisca!" he exclaimed.

She raised her head but didn't speak.

"What's wrong with her?" he demanded.

"They gave her some drugs to make her more obedient. Apparently, she's having some type of reaction to them. You need to get her into ER as soon as possible. Tommasa too."

Carlos hadn't seen anyone besides his daughter. Now he turned to look at Tommasa. "Who is this?"

Tommasa looked him in the eye and gave him her name.

"You appear to have survived better than my daughter. Why is that?"

Tommasa shrugged. "I seem to have a natural resistance to the drug. Its effect wears off quicker for me. Are you going to take me too?"

"Yes, of course," he said. "I beg your pardon for not noticing you earlier—I'm afraid I didn't notice anyone but Francisca." As he spoke, he lifted his daughter off Ava's sled and carried her toward the open door of his sled. "I'm going to lay her down in the cargo space," he told Tommasa. "You can have the other seat."

After a glance at Ava, Tommasa followed him.

"Let's get out of here," Randal said. His sled rose overhead, and he fired a pulse blast at the canopy of leaves directly above them, creating a hole. Devon and the two girls followed him through it.

Ava looked back and saw Carlos hit the building with a more powerful blast, reducing it to cinders and blowing a hole in the roof of the basement. He fired again and the basement exploded. He turned and followed them up above the canopy.

The Red Conclave's standard mode of operations was to keep a low profile, but after the attack on the shed they sent a couple of sleds in pursuit of the rescue party.

Randal and Devon dropped behind to engage their pursuers. "Go, Judith," he ordered. "We'll meet you at the house as soon as we take care of these guys."

"Okay," Judith said, adding to Ava, "Dammit I don't have any weapons! I need to get him to add a pulse blaster to *my* sled."

AT SWORDS POINT

JUDITH AND Ava stopped by the house Tash and Devon were living in to pick up Licorice and Sunrise. Ava picked up an extra bottle and a packet of soft kitten food for Sunrise before she sent the vet bot back to her parent's house.

"I'm going to check on the girls before I head home," she told Judith.

"You can tell Mom I'm at the hospital when she asks."

"Hummn," Judith eyed her elder sister. "Can I tell her about you and Carlos?"

Ava shrugged, "It doesn't matter. You can tell her how I feel if you want; it might stop her from attempting to match me with cretins. I can't vouch for Carlos's feelings, if he has any."

Judith nodded. "It's about time she clued in."

When Ava arrived at the hospital, she was annoyed to find Tommasa still sitting in the ER waiting room to be seen.

"Why haven't they seen you yet?" she asked the girl.

Tommasa gave her a lop-sided smile. "Not high on their priority list, I guess."

"We'll just see about that," Ava said.

She marched up to the admissions desk, demanding, "Why hasn't that girl been seen yet?"

The clerk eyed her warily. She could see the steam rising as Ava glared at her. "What is her name?" she asked.

"Tommasa Elena de'Ricci," Ava said enunciating each word carefully.

The clerk hastily consulted her terminal. "She's a minor. We can't treat her without a parent's permission,"

"Did you com her parents?" Ava demanded.

"Yes, over a half hour ago; they haven't responded."

"Well, com them again!" Ava said impatiently. "Or better yet, give *me* the number and *I'll* com them."

"That won't be necessary," a smooth tenor voice interjected.

Ava turned to look at him. She saw a tall, slim man with an olive complexion and grey eyes in a dressy doublet and pantaloons. His pompous air made her dislike him on sight. "Who are you? You're too young to be Tommasa's father."

"Thank God for that. My name is Giuseppe Capitano. I'm aide to Representative Giorgio de'Ricci, the minor's father."

"Did you bring permission for the doctor's to see her?"

He frowned at her. "Who are you?"

"I'm Ava Garneys. I am one of the people who rescued *Tommasa*," she informed him, stressing the girl's name.

He turned back to the admission's clerk, dismissing Ava, who could feel herself coming to a slow boil.

Capitano handed the clerk a sheaf of papers. "This is a document renouncing their guardianship of the minor, Tommasa Elena de'Ricci to the Child Welfare Department. As soon as a representative arrives and accepts guardianship, I assume a doctor can see her."

"Give me those papers," Ava demanded.

The clerk meekly handed them over. Capitano glared at the clerk. "Those are supposed to be private, "he said.

Ava ignored the bi-play and began reading through them until she found where the words Child Welfare Office had been typed in. She crossed it out and wrote in her own name. "Send for the Notary," she ordered the clerk, who hastily got on the com with the admissions office.

"The notary will be here in about five minutes," she said.

Capitano frowned at Ava. "Why do you want become her guardian?" he asked in honest surprise.

Ava glared at him. "Someone needs to. She's a brave young lady. Smart too."

The Notary, a brisk, bright eyed little woman about fifty, came up. "I hear you have documents that have to be notarized?"

"Yes," Ava handed her the pages.

"Come over here," The woman said, moving to an empty desk behind the Admission's Clerk.

She frowned over the papers. "I see the parent's signatures consigning the girl to social service has been scratched out. I'm afraid that means the transfer to your guardianship will need to be re-notarized, Miss Garneys."

"I'm betting Capitano can do it as their agent, can't you?" Ava said.

"Yes," he said, "but I'm reluctant to do it without at least a verbal okay from my boss."

He met Ava's deadly stare and said hastily, "Give me a moment to com him."

He stepped away from the desk, creating a Cone of Silence around himself while he made the com.

They could see him nod several times before he closed the com and the cone. "Yes, I can agree to her guardianship on my bosses behalf. Where do I sign?"

The notary took their ID's snapping a vid still of them which she attached to the file. "Sign here," she said.

They both signed, then added their DNA to the signature. The Notary handed them each a copy of the paperwork and packed her things into a sealed pouch that could only be opened by her DNA signature and left for the Admissions Office.

Ava turned to the Admissions Clerk, "Now, get this girl seen!"

"Yes ma'am," the clerk hastily called the triage nurse, pointing to Tommasa.

As Ava was following them to the exam room, she ran into Carlos.

"How is Francisca?" she asked.

"They pumped her stomach and gave her something to counteract the drugs she was given. She's asleep. Could I impose on you to sit with her until she wakes up? I need to go release Coudet from the cage I was keeping him in (I told him I'd let him go as soon as I had my daughter back). I don't want her to wake up alone."

Ava nodded. "I'll need you to tell admissions it's okay to put Tommasa in the same room. I just signed up to be her guardian. I'll tell you about *that* later."

"I'll do that. Thank you." Unexpectedly, he brushed her cheek with a kiss, before heading toward the admissions desk.

Ava stared after him a moment in astonishment, before turning to go

look for where they had taken
Tommasa.

Randal and Devon were already at
the cave when Carlos arrived.

"Hello," he said in surprise.
"What are you doing here?"

"We wanted to volunteer to act as
your seconds when Coudet challenges
you," Randal told him.

Carlos had friends from the old
days he could ask, but that would've
involved a lengthy explanation and he
didn't want to do that.

"Thank you, I accept," Carlos told
them.

Carlos let Coudet out of the out
of the cage. Coudet Eyed him warily.
"What happens now?" The man asked.

"I take you back to town. I will
of course expect to receive a
challenge from you over this. My
seconds will meet with yours when and
where they please."

Coudet looked at him in silence long moment before he spoke. "I have less of a beef with you over this then I do with the man who gave the order to take your daughter. He must've known how you would react. He set me up to take the fall for it."

"Who ordered you to take my daughter?" Carlos asked softly.

Coudet shrugged. "His name is Jerome Redglove, you probably know him. I understand he's an up-and-coming politician. He is also the head of the Red Conclave."

Carlos frowned. "Why would he order my daughter taken?" he asked suspiciously.

Coudet lifted his hands. "The word that came down through the organization, is he wanted to teach you a lesson about going after the Red Conclave members so hard when you prosecute them."

"I take it that means you don't intend to challenge me?"

Coudet looked relieved. "That's right."

"It looks like I'm going hunting," Carlos said.

MOTHER BEAR

THE DOCTOR frowned at Ava. "You are the child's guardian?"

"Yes," Ava replied. Tommasa looked up in surprise.

"She seems to be doing better physically than the other patient rescued from the kidnappers," he said, "But I'd like to keep her overnight for observation anyway."

Ava nodded, "That's fine if she and Francisca Santana share a room. They were rescued together, and I think they will be more comfortable if they are together during their stay."

The admissions nurse objected. "Francisca Santana is in a private room. You can't just opt for your daughter to join her—"

"I have her father's permission," Ava retorted. "Would you like me to com him so you can speak to him personally?"

"That won't be necessary," The doctor, whose name tag read Dr. Baradeau said. "Mr. Santana spoke to me about this before he left the hospital. Those are his wishes as well. Please see that a bed is brought up to the room."

"Yes sir," the admissions nurse replied, dropping her eyes. Ava could hear the carefully controlled resentment in her voice.

Dr. Baradeau seemed to hear it also, because he added, "I'm sure you'll accomplish this with your usual speed and efficiency Mary. I know you are one of the mainstays of keeping this place running so well."

Mary flushed a little. "Thank you Dr. Baradeau."

"Henri, please," he said, smiling at her.

"Give me about twenty minutes to arrange things Ms. Garneys," she said, and bustled out of the room.

Another nurse came in, closing the privacy curtains behind her. "Let's get you out of those clothes and into a hospital gown. I've brought a bag for your things." As she spoke, she shook out a blue gown open at the back.

Tommasa slid out of the bed on the side away from the nurse. She unbuckled the pistol belt and handed it off to Ava, who slung it over her shoulder.

The nurse's eyebrows rose when she saw the weapon. Tommasa had been lying with a sheet across her hips, so she hadn't seen it before. She opened her mouth to say something, met Ava's flat stare and changed her mind.

"Must be nice to intimidate people with that thousand-yard stare; I'll need to practice more before I can do that."

Ava sank down into a chair to wait for them to come to take her new daughter upstairs. "You'll get there," she said.

Sunrise, who had been asleep until now began to wiggle her way out of the pouch.

"Oh," Tommasa exclaimed, "What is it? It looks like a catamount, but it has fur."

"This is Sunrise. She is a catamount," Ava replied. "Just a different variety than those who live down here in the tropics. The correct name for her variety is Hairy Catamount."

"She looks like a kitten."

"She is. I rescued her and her mom from a pack of Kevlars. Her mom didn't make it."

"I guess I need to say thank you for rescuing me from social services," Tommasa said. Privately she was wondering if Ava saw her the way she saw the catamount. She looked into the woman's eyes and found Ava was watching her with amused comprehension.

"No, I don't regard you as a homeless waif in need of rescuing; I think in time you would have figured a way out of the fix you were in. You're resourceful and tough."

Tommasa blushed up to the roots of her hair. "Are you a mind reader?" she demanded. "How did you know what I was thinking?"

"No," Ava chuckled, "I don't read minds, so you won't need to wrap your head in tinfoil. But I *am* very good at reading people. Most of the time."

"Is that why you never got married?" Tommasa asked.

"Pretty much," Ava admitted wryly. "That and the fact I just didn't like any of them."

"You could have let social services take me, but you didn't. Why not?"

"I guess because I used to be you. Only my parents were supportive. I felt you had the right to know what that felt like. No matter how badly I behaved, I always knew my parents wouldn't throw me away. I'm sorry, but I just don't understand people like that."

Tears filled Tommasa's eyes, and she bit her lip. "They hate me," she whispered. "I never understood why they didn't give me up for adoption."

"You're their daughter!" Ava said, scandalized.

"That's just it—I'm not. Oh, they stood as mother and father to me but I'm the daughter of my father's sister. She was raped. After she had me, she killed herself. To avoid a scandal, they took me as their daughter."

Ava had her mouth open for a blistering condemnation about the elder de'Riccis, but an orderly coming in to move Tommasa upstairs to Francisca's room prevented her.

The orderlies had shifted Francisca's bed out of the center of the room to make space for Tommasa's, which a nurse was just now making up. Francisca had apparently slept through the entire thing.

"How long before she wakes up?" Ava asked.

The duty nurse, whose name tag read Borgia, was in her early thirties. Her light brown hair was caught back in a bun. Her nurses cap had wings with a blue stripe. She had a sturdy body and a pleasant smile. She consulted the medi-tab at the foot of the bed. "It might be several hours. She is suffering from exhaustion, malnutrition and dehydration."

She went to the foot of Tommasa's bed and picked up her medi-tab. "The Doctor ordered you be given eight ounces of juice every three hours. We have orange, tomato and pineapple. Which would you prefer?"

"Ah—orange juice to start," Tommasa replied.

"Coming right up," the nurse bustled out.

Ava's com beeped. It was Judith. "Hey, where are you?" her sister demanded.

"I'm in Tommasa's and Francisca's room at the hospital," Ava replied. "Who wants to know?" she asked suspiciously.

Judith laughed. "Well, me for one. But Mom will want to know as well."

"So, tell her. It's not a secret. Ummn, you can also tell her I sighed up to be Tommasa's guardian after those bastards who claim to be parents washed their hands of her. Ask her to get the room next to mine ready. And when you bring me a change of clothes, go by and pick up a couple of things for Tommasa a well."

"Sure, what size does she wear?"

"Hang on, I'll ask her. Tommasa, my sister's going to pick up some clothes for you and she wants to know your sizes."

"Size 14, I think."

Ava relayed this information to Judith. She turned back to Tommasa.

"She wants your shoe size and your bra and panties as well. Here, this is silly, you talk to her." She handed her com bracelet over to the girl.

Tommasa handed it back when Judith hung up. "Who is Aunt Carmen?"

"Aunt Carmen is a force of nature. She's probably in her eighties, but no one knows for sure, and she isn't saying. If Judith is taking her shopping for you, there is no telling what they might bring for you to wear."

For the first time in a long time, Tommasa laughed. "She sounds like fun. Anything will be better that what they gave us at the plantation!"

Sunrise, whom Ava had let loose to explore began scratching at the bathroom door. "Uh-Oh, I bet she needs to pee or potty. Excuse me while I find something to serve as a litter box."

Ava opened the bathroom door and went in. Sunrise darted past her. Not finding what she was looking for, she finally climbed in the shower stall which looked huge for a litter box, but she used it anyway. Ava sighed and cleaned it up. She knew from experience the kitten would be hungry, so she dug a bottle out of her pouch.

"Would you mind feeding her while I find something to put her solid food in?" she asked.

"Sure, just show me what to do," Tommasa said, reaching for Sunrise.

Ava handed her the bottle of formula and Sunrise latched on eagerly.

"Wow!" Tommasa exclaimed, "She's a lot stronger than I thought she would be. How old is she?"

"The vet said about four weeks."

Tamara arrived before Judith and Aunt Carmen. "Your vet bot said Sunrise would need more formula and solid food. I didn't know how long you would be kept here so I brought it with your clothes. Ava, introduce me to my new granddaughter."

Ava smiled, "Tommasa, this is my mother, Tamara Garneys."

"Ah, hello," Tommasa said.

"Hello, dear," Tamara came over and gave her a hug, much to Tommasa's surprise; she had expected Ava's parents to be standoffish. Such a warm welcome gave her a funny feeling in her tummy.

"Judith and Aunt Carmen went shopping for Tommasa's clothes," Ava told her.

"Well, if they get something really awful, I'll have the seamstress-bot run you up something you like better," Tamara promised.

Tommasa blinked in surprise when Judith and Aunt Carmen bustled in. Judith, she had met at the plantation when she was rescued. Ava's Aunt Carmen was a new experience for her. The woman was tiny, with her white hair in a pixie cut. In defiance of the current fashions for older women, she wore skin-tight leggings in a virulent pink, a tight bustier of the same color and a blouse covered in ruffles.

Aunt Carmen gave Ava a hug and came over to the bed. After looking Tommasa over carefully, she pronounced. "She'll do. Welcome to the family Tommasa. I'm your Aunt Carmen.

"Thank you," Tommasa said. Ava had been right; being around Aunt Carmen was like being in the center of a hurricane.

"Judith says you are a shooter. Where's your gun?"

"Ah—in that bag with my clothes."

Without asking permission, Aunt Carmen went to the bag and rummaged through it. She pulled out the ragged, dirty t-shirt with a moue of distaste. "Throw that rag away," she tossed the shirt at Judith who caught it and obediently stuffed it in the rooms trash can. Carmen pulled out the pistol and examined it, "Hummn, not bad. Hasn't been cleaned in a while though. Where's your cleaning kit?"

"I don't have one. I just took that one off a dead man."

If she had intended to shock the older woman, it failed. Carmen nodded approvingly. "The one Judith shot? That was a smart move. Never leave an armed foe behind you, even if he appears dead."

"Yes, ma'am," Tommasa said.

Carmen gave a bray of a laugh. "Don't Ma'am, me girl—makes me feel older than I am. I'm just Carmen or Aunt Carmen if you prefer."

"Yes, Aunt Carmen," Tommasa said meekly, and the old woman nodded approvingly.

The charge nurse entered the room, a militant look in her eye. "Too many visitors in here," she declared. "These girls need to rest. I'm afraid I'll have to ask you to leave."

Carmen turned on her, the light of battle in her eye. Before she could open her mouth, Tamara and Judith each took her arm and hustled her toward the door. "We'll come back later," Judith said.

As they were leaving, Carlos walked in. Nurse Borgia frowned at him. "Sir, I'm sorry, but visiting hours—"

"This is Francisca's father," Ava intervened.

"Oh, in that case, it's fine," she said. "Your daughter should be waking up soon, Mr. Santana. I need to take her vitals though, so if you'll step back a little."

She took a portable scanner out of her pocket and ran it over Francisca. When it beeped, she aimed it at the Medi-tab at the foot of the bed before restoring it to her pocket. She straightened the bed sheet and tucked it around the girl before going to Tommasa and doing the same thing.

"Would you like another orange juice or maybe something different this time?"

"Could I have pineapple?"

"Absolutely. Just give me a couple of minutes to enter the readings on the hospital computer."

She bustled out.

Carlos pulled a chair close to the bed and took his daughter's hand.

Francisca's eyelashes fluttered, and she asked, "Daddy?" in a hopeful voice.

"I'm here sweetie," he said.

Francisca sat up and threw herself at him, bursting in to tears. All the alarms on her bed went off when Carlos picked her up and sat her on his lap, cuddling her.

"I'm so sorry, Daddy," she blubbered. "I was too stupid to listen to you. I thought he really liked me, but it was all a lie."

"Yes Darling, I know. This was my fault as much as yours; I should have protected you better. Coudet was under orders to take you. I'm sorry, baby."

Nurse Borgia and several orderlies entered the room at a run.

"Her monitors are all going off—Oh, I see," she said, when she saw Francisca sitting in her father's lap. She came to the bed and shut off the alarm. She tapped her shoulder tab and told it, "Cancel Code Blue."

She pulled a box of tissues out of a drawer and handed them to Carlos. Francisca took several and wiped her face and blew her nose.

A pert looking dietician poked her head in the door, asking, "Okay to bring in the dinner trays now?"

"Yes, go ahead," Nurse Borgia replied.

"Dr. Baradeau prescribed a light meal for both of you. If you can tolerate it you can have something more substantial for breakfast. I have a list of choices for you to choose from. Just put in your order."

She pulled Tommasa's table across her lap and set out a covered plate of Mashed tubers, a meat blob, and something green, to be chased with an eight-ounce glass of milk. It was impossible to tell what the original items had been, since they had all been through a blender until they were a smooth pulp.

Tommasa eyed the plate in revulsion. "This looks like baby food—do I have to eat it?"

The dietician laughed. "Just until we see if your system can tolerate it. How long has it been since you ate a real meal?"

"Quite a while," Tommasa admitted grudgingly. She lifted a forkful of the tubers, hoping it was potatoes and put it in her mouth.

The dietician turned to Francisca. "Would you like to eat sitting in your Daddy's lap, dear?"

When Francisca nodded, she adjusted the table and set out the same meal she had given Tommasa, with the instructions, "Just eat until you fee full. Don't force it."

Francisca fell asleep again after dinner. Carlos laid her in the bed.

"Ava, I hate to impose on you again, but Coudet gave me the name of the man who ordered my daughter taken. I need to find him. Could you stay until I get back?"

"I'll probably be here anyway," she assured him. "If they let her come home before you get back, do you want me to take her home with me and Tommasa?"

"Yes, please. If she wakes up tell her I've gone hunting the man who ordered her taken so I can make sure he doesn't do this again."

"Of course," Ava replied.

RIDE THE MAN DOWN

CARLOS WAS SURPRISED to find Devon and Randal waiting in the sled park when he arrived there.

Devon was just finishing a Com to Tash when he arrived.

"What are you two doing here?"

"We're your Seconds, remember?" Randal said.

"This kind of hunt can get nasty; did you tell your ladies what you are going to be doing?"

"Yeah," Devon replied. "Tash isn't happy about it, but she agreed it needed to be done."

"Judith told me if I got hurt just before the wedding she would skin me," Randal added. "How is your daughter doing?"

Carlos smiled. "She cried all over me then ate dinner and fell asleep. Ava's watching her."

"Where do you want to start?" Devon asked.

"We'll start at his office first. If that doesn't work out, we'll have to go to his home."

Redglove's office manager, Eulalia Brinckhurst, was a woman in her Late thirties with carefully made-up face and hands. Her Auburn hair was done up in a neat twist. She denied any knowledge of her boss's whereabouts. "He's on vacation," she said. "He wanted to get completely away for a few days while the council is in recess."

"When do you expect him back?" Carlos asked.

"The council is due to meet next month. Shall I see if I can schedule you an appointment?"

"Yes," Carlos crossed his arms and sat on the edge of the desk. Randal and Devon imitated him. "We'll wait while you do that."

She gave him and his two satellites an exasperated glance before stalking over to the virtual terminal and calling up the calendar. "I'm sorry, Mr. Redglove's schedule seems to be full for the next two months. If there is an opening, I will call you."

"I'll remember what you said," Carlos told her. "C'mon gentlemen, we'll see if his household knows anything more."

Eulalia waited until they were out of earshot before she contacted her boss. She was a longtime member of

153

the Red Conclave, having been indoctrinated as a teenager.

"Carlos Santana and two younger men just left," she reported. "I told them you were on vacation, and you didn't have an opening in your calendar for at least two months after you return."

"Excellent. That should hold him."

"I don't think so—he's gone to your home to look for you there. I don't think he will give up, sir, and—"

"And what?"

"I did a little research on him. Before he took up the law as a profession, he was a bounty hunter. A good one."

"Alright, I'll take it from here."

"Yes sir."

Unknown to Eulalia, Devon had planted one of his listening/recording devices under the lip of her desk. The three of them heard every word said by Eulalia and Redglove.

"Think it's worthwhile to go to his house?" Randal asked.

"Of course; we don't want them to suspect we've planted a listening device." Carlos replied. "Where can I get some of those?" he asked Devon.

"From me. They are my own invention," Devon replied. "They can also be programmed for tracking, and the nanobots are designed to blend in with their surroundings. I only brought a few of them with me for Randal to show to the Black Templars. Just tell me how many you want, and I'll send them to you."

"I'll do that," Carlos said.

JEANNINE Dryden had been Jerome Redglove's housekeeper ever since the death of her mother, who had

155

previously held the post. She knew the rules under which the house operated. Since her boss hadn't told her where he was going or how long he intended to be gone, she knew she was to deny all knowledge of those things. So, when Carlos Santana came asking questions, she greeted him pleasantly with the words, "Mr. Redglove isn't home. I don't know when he will be here."

Randal and Devon simply watched in silence. Randal had his tab out, checking for other properties in Redglove's name.

"Is his wife here? I'd like to speak to her, if I may."

"I'm sorry sir, but Mrs. Redglove went to Dancing Beach for several weeks."

"Will her husband be joining her there?"

"I don't know. He didn't share his intentions with the staff."

"Thank you for your time, Miss Dryden."

Carlos walked back down the steps to where the others waited.

"Where is the Dancing Beach? I don't think I've ever heard of it," Devon asked.

"It's a day's journey south of here, even by sled. It's where the Parchester River meets the Langstino Sea."

"Does it dance?"

Randal laughed. "No but the Blue Whisps come out at dawn and dusk to sing and dance. I've never seen it myself, but I'm told it's quite charming."

Devon frowned at little. "Are they sentient?"

Randal shrugged. "Our scientists say no, but we don't know that much about them. They are aquatic mammals we think but that's just from observation. There is a scientist station located near Dancing Beach whose sole interest is in studying them."

"Randal found a list of properties owned by Redglove. Are we going to check them out?"

"Yes," Carlos nodded. "If he's not at any of them, we might need to speak to Mrs. Redglove."

He opened the door on the side of his big sled, stepping inside just as a bullet from a pulse rifle clipped the side of the vehicle. "Down!" he bellowed. Randal and Devon both hit the protection shield on their sleds and turned them to face the direction the shot came from. Two more shots ricocheted off the center of their shielding with an ear-splitting whine.

They gunned their sleds and took off toward where the shots came from.

The sniper, Tobias Tudor, was too old a hand to stay in the spot he shot from. He mounted his waiting sled, invoking the stealth program and took off. He had managed to tag Carlos's sled earlier so he knew he could find him again.

"He's gone," Randal reported in disgust.

"He was here though," Devon had dismounted and was examining the ground around the area. The Blue Moon Militia, the group who protected the Town of Laughing Mountain, taught tracking as well as other skills. Devon hadn't gotten high marks, but he wasn't too bad either. "From the tracks where he parked, I'd say he was riding a one-man sled."

"Did you say you had located property records showing Redglove's ownership?" Carlos asked.

"Yes, I have them here," Devon unloaded several files to their coms. "For a criminal mastermind, he has very poor cyber security."

Carlos looked up from studying the list in surprise. "That's interesting, considering our people in IT don't seem to be able to find him on our planet net. Did you find anything interesting besides property records?"

Devon laughed. "After dealing with Earth-Gov's stuff, these folks are a lark. When I was in there, I grabbed the whole enchilada—finances, what they are into, property records and safe houses; let me sort through it for you and then I'll send it off."

"But not while we're on the way to someplace," Randal said,

"Hey—that only happened once," Devon protested. "Tash insisted I put a lockout so I couldn't access it if I was moving, anyway."

"Send us the list of safe houses," Carlos requested. "If he's hiding out until his people can stop me looking for him, that's probably where he'll be."

The closest safe house was in an isolated area on the other side of Grantois Lake, a freshwater lake within a dormant volcanic caldera just outside the capital city.

"We've got time before it gets dark, let's check that one out first," Randal suggested.

It was late afternoon when they reached the first house, a two story, octagon shaped building with a deep porch which served as a deck on the second story. Like all human-built structures on Barsoom, it floated on a plasticrete slab anchored to the ground by plasti-steel pilons which could be raised in times of flooding.

Frowning, all three men scanned the house. "I don't read anything," Randal said. "Do you?"

"I don't either," Devon said. "He could be in a shielded room or basement though."

"In that case, wouldn't the shielded area show as a blank spot?"

"Not necessarily," Devon replied. "It depends on how good the shielding is, I've seen some that cover the blank spot with images of the surrounding area."

"It could be a trap." Carlos stepped down from his sled. "The two of you stay out here while I check it for booby traps. Be ready to vamoose in a hurry if I call it."

"You're no fun," Randal complained.

"What's that?" Devon asked, pointing at the rod Carlos was carrying. "This is a dousing tool left over from my bounty hunting days," Carlos told them. "It scans for explosive materials."

Carlos approached the structure cautiously. He aimed the dousing tool at the ground in front of him, checking for trip wires and land mines.

"So far, so good," he said. He touched the handle on the door and the dousing rod made a contented hum.

"It's not locked," He stood to one side when he pushed on the door. It swung open with a creaking sound.

"Creepy," Devon remarked.

Carlos scanned the entryway, and the dousing rod changed its tune. "It's found something," he said. He tapped the rod on the doorsill and there was an ominous click.

Carlos sprang back and ran for his sled. "Run!" he shouted.

As they sped away from the house, the shock wave from the explosion hit them, tossing all three sleds around like confetti. Behind them rose a great fireball.

"Wow! Randal exclaimed. "I don't know about the two of you, but I vote we head for home and hit the other houses in the morning. I want to pick up a couple of items from Templar headquarters before we search the other properties."

"A good idea," Carlos agreed.

MEDEA'S CHOICE

THE GIRLS were just finishing breakfast, a more substantial meal this time, and Ava was cleaning up Sunrise's latest trip to use the shower as a litter box when Elinor Crawley entered the room.

"Well, I see you survived your latest tantrum," she told Francisca.

The dietitian, who was measuring how much Tommasa had eaten of the meal of cream of wheat, gelatin and a large juice, frowned at the comment.

When Ava and Sunrise left the bathroom, Elinor gave a tiny scream. "A rat! There's a rat in here! What kind of a hospital is this? You're infested with vermin! Get it away from me!"

"Sunrise isn't a rat!" declared Tommasa indignantly. "She's a catamount. She's Ava's pet."

"I think she's cute. I'm going to ask Daddy if I can have one for a pet," Francisca said.

"Not going to happen, you spoiled little brat," Elinor told her, with an arrogant toss of her head. "As soon as Carlos and I get married you're going to St. Ophelia's finishing school as a boarder. They'll put an end to these little stunts!"

"You're a liar! Daddy might have screwed you a couple of times, but he won't marry you!"

"Oh, don't try to play with the big girls; you haven't got a say in this. He'll marry me and get shut of you."

Francisca's lip trembled. "That's not true. Daddy loves me. He's not going to marry you because—because he's going to marry someone else," she announced in desperation.

"You lying little bitch! It's time somebody taught you some manners—" Elinor took a step toward Francisca with her hand raised, obviously intending to slap the younger girl.

The dietitian had stood rooted with her mouth open in shock during this dialog, not believing Elinor would slap her patient. Ava, who had a better understanding of Elinor's character, hastily handed Sunrise to Tommasa and moved to grab Elinor's wrist. She caught the other woman's arm before the blow landed, and twisted, hard. Elinor teetered on her stiletto heels, lost her balance and ended up on her butt on the floor.

"Well, it won't be you today," Ava informed her.

Elinor let loose with a string of curses which would have made a deckhand proud, as she scrambled to her feet. Tommasa laughed. The dietitian finally had the presence of mind to hit the panic button on the bed, and the charge nurse came rushing in.

"What happened here?" She demanded.

Elinor promptly burst into tears and declared, "She attacked me!" She pointed at Ava.

"That's a lie!" Francisca cried out. "Ava kept you from hitting me after you called me names!"

The nurse frowned. "Who tried to hit you?" she asked Francisca.

"She did," Francisca declared, pointing at Elinor.

Nurse Borgia looked at Pava. "Did you see this?"

"Yes, I did. Miss Santana is telling the truth; The slap didn't hit home because Ms. Garneys intervened."

"That is a serious charge. I will have to report it to hospital administration." She looked at Ava. "Are you willing to testify Ms. Garneys?"

"Yes, of course."

"So will I; I saw it too," Tommasa interjected,

"I never touched the little bitch!" Elinor said.

Nurse Borgia smiled grimly. "The intent is enough to file charges, Ms. Crawley."

"Damn you! This isn't over." Elinor glared at Ava and stomped out,

Ava watched her leave, hands on her hips. "Good God—what can Carlos be thinking?"

"Maybe she's fantastically good in bed?" Tommasa suggested.

"She'd have to be," Ava snorted out a laugh.

"Is it okay to come in?" Judith asked from the doorway. "I just passed the Wicked Witch of The West storming off down the hall. What happened?"

"That's good; I'll have to remember that one," Tommasa said with a giggle.

"You missed all the excitement," her sister told her.

"You don't think Daddy will really marry her do you?" Francisca asked, tears in her voice.

"I doubt it, Hon," Ava said reassuringly. "Your daddy is too smart to let what's in his pants rule his head."

"Not to change the subject," Judith remarked, "But I've brought clothes." She handed Ava and Tommasa bags of clothes. She drew a third one out of her tote for Francisca. "I had to guess at your sizes," she told her apologetically.

"Where did you ditch Aunt Carmen?" Ava asked, pulling out an off-white blouse with a blue striped bustier and a pair of form fitting pants in the same color. The panties and bra she left in the bag.

Tommasa pulled out an outfit like Ava's but in yellow with brilliant red stripes. "Thank you," the girl said to Judith. She turned to Francisca. "What color is yours?"

"Yes, Thank you, Miss Garneys." Francisca said, staring at the pink and white striped pants and bustier.

"Judith, please; Miss Garneys is too formal. Your daddy is a good friend of our family."

Aunt Carmen stalked into the room, muttering, "Bunch of damn fools!"

"Did they let you bring them in?" Judith asked.

"Yes, they did. I had to call the top administrator to get him to okay it, though. Luckily I went to school with him. He's always been a little afraid of me."

"Well, this is a hospital," Judith reminded her.

"Hah!" Carmen snorted. "I saw you only had a pistol Tommasa, so I brought you this."

It was a poniard in a leather tooled sheath with a finely carved handle. Tommasa took the dagger out to see it. "Oh, WoW! This is beautiful," she said. "Thank you."

Carmen also dropped a gun cleaner case on the bed. "Don't forget to clean that pistol!"

She walked over to Francisca, who had been watching enviously and dropped another poniard and a holstered pistol.

Francisca looked up at her with shining eyes, "These are for me?"

"Well, I figured you didn't have one either." Carmen shrugged. "If you don't know how to use them, come and see me. I'll teach you. That goes for you too," she told Tommasa.

"I can shoot a pistol," Tommasa said. "I've never had any training with a knife though."

"As soon as they let you out of this bird house, we can start your lessons," Carmen promised.

` Once she exited the hospital, Elinor called her friend Adeline to complain about Francisca. "You said you were going to get rid of her! He found her; she's in the hospital, getting better! What am I going to do about that?"

"Do you know when she's being released?"

"They wouldn't tell me. I told them I was Santana's fiancé, but it was no go. If he isn't there to pick her up when she's released, she's supposed to go home with Ava Garneys."

"Isn't he with her?"

"It seems not. Just before I went into the room, I heard Ava Garneys telling the kid her daddy had gone man-hunting."

"For Coudet?" Prowd asked sharply.

"Apparently Coudet told Santana he was under orders to take the girl, and Santana went off with blood in his eye. He used to be a bounty hunter; you know."

"Hummn, I'll have to get back to you. In the meantime, try to find out if Santana's alone on his hunting trip."

DAUGHTER OF
DARKNESS

WHEN THE news came down that the girls could go home, Carlos still hadn't returned. Francisca's lip trembled.

"I don't want to go home if nobody's there."

"Carlos knew that" Ava told her. "That's why you're coming home with us."

She commed her mother to pick them up, but they were still waiting for transports when Tamara came upstairs. "What's the holdup?" She demanded.

Ava opened her mouth to answer just as two orderlies pushing cushioned chairs entered. Like most vehicles on Barsoom, the powered chairs used by the hospital, ran on Gregor crystals. It was the same principle as the sleds, except the controls were in the handles located on the top of the chair backs.

"All ready to go?" One of them asked with a smile.

"Am I ever!" Tommasa said, planting herself in one of the chairs.

She looked over at Francisca impatiently. "What are you waiting for? Let's go!"

"Francisca looked at Ava for reassurance. "Are you sure it's okay?"

Tamara came and gave her a reassuring hug. "Of course, dear. You're very welcome at our house. Your daddy is a very old friend of ours."

The orderlies brought them down to the hospital valet area where the valet in charge sent the signal for the Garneys big sled to come to them. He frowned, looked at the code key Tamara had given him, and keyed it in again.

"What's wrong?" Ava asked.

"Nothing, it was just a little slow responding. You might want to get it checked out by a repair place."

When the sled, disguised to look like a roomy carriage, arrived, the valet reached for the door. Ava had been feeling uneasy ever since the valet said the controls were slow to respond. Agustin Garneys kept all their home equipment controls, including the sleds, in perfect condition. The uneasy feeling coalesced into action.

"Stop!" She shouted, drawing her pistol.

"What is it? What's wrong?" Tamara asked.

"I'm not sure," her older daughter said. "Tommasa, draw your weapon. You're my backup. The rest of you get back."

Proud to be trusted, Tommasa got out of the chair and positioned herself a little behind and to one side. "I'm ready," she said.

"Alright, go ahead and open the door," Ava told the valet. "Be sure you're standing behind it when you do."

Gingerly, he did so. When the door swung open, it was followed by a striking viper. Ava fired at the snake as it fell forward. Her shot was followed a few second later by Tommasa's. The rest of the body followed the head down. For several seconds it flailed around before it realized it was dead.

"Good job," Ava told her foster daughter, and was rewarded by a glowing smile.

"How did you know something was wrong?" Tamara asked.

"Dad keeps our equipment in perfect condition, Mom," she replied. She didn't share with her mother her suspicion the attack might have been intended to draw Carlos away from hunting for whoever sent the order to take Francisca.

"I'm not riding in that until it's been cleaned," Tamara announced. "Call us a cab please," she told the valet.

"Yes, ma'am," he said. "If you'll give me the address of your repair shop, I'll call one as soon as this one has cleared the area."

Tamara gave it to him, and the carriage rose into the air. It was about twenty feet off the ground when it blew up. Everyone ducked, Ava and Tamara instinctively shielding the two girls. The valet hit the storm shielding, preventing most of the burning debris from landing in the immediate area. The force field had originally been designed as a shield from inclement weather, but it was just as effective against falling debris.

Hospital security rushed outside, demanding to know what had just happened. In short order, they had cleared the area of spectators and shepherded the Garneys family back inside the hospital.

Ava was giving them her statement, when having received a garbled account from his wife about the incident, Agustin Garneys arrived, breathing fire and under the impression his wife and daughter were being detained.

"They aren't being detained or arrested!" The beleaguered head of hospital security told him. "We're only trying to learn what happened."

"You can send someone to my house to ask your questions," Agustin said militantly. "This place isn't safe! C'mon girls. I've got a carriage outside I *know* hasn't been tampered with!" With that he hustled all of them out to the carriage.

"Alright, what's going on?" he fixed Ava with stare that would have pinned a beetle specimen to Styrofoam.

"This is only a guess," she said, "but I think whoever ordered Francisca taken bit off more than he can chew. Carlos went after him—this might be an attempt to draw him off the trail."

"I see," Agustin said. He saw the anxious look on Francisca's face and patted her hand reassuringly. "We'll keep you safe until Carlos catches him."

"You're awfully sure he will find him," Tamara remarked.

Agustin nodded. "I am. You might not remember, but he used to have quite a name as a bounty hunter before he took up the law. He'll get him."

The three hunters were on the way back to Savona when all three of the men's coms sounded incoming messages. Randal and Devon's callers were Tash and Judith, demanding an update on the search for the man who ordered Francisca taken. Carlos's got a com from Agustin.

"We have your daughter safe with us," the older man said. "I would have appreciated a com before you landed my family in a nest of stinging beetles though."

"What do you mean? What happened?" Carlos demanded.

"Someone planted a pit viper in my carriage while it was in the hospital parking lot. Then when it took off for the repair shop, it blew up—"

"Is anyone hurt?" Carlos demanded.

"We got lucky. Ava and Tommasa shot the viper. It didn't get a chance to bite anyone. Fortunately, my wife is too fastidious to ride in a carriage smeared with reptile, so no one was in it when it blew up. Just what kind of trouble are you in, son?"

Carlos grimaced. "I've been going after the Red Conclave hard prosecuting them. They decided to teach me a lesson and kidnapped my daughter. If I don't get the man behind the order, I might as well give up as District Attorney."

Agustin nodded. "You get your man. Francisca will be safe with us. As soon as we got home from the hospital, I set the house in security lockdown."

"Thank you, Agustin. As soon as I get some breathing room, I'll com my daughter. And thank Ava for me—I don't think we could have found Francisca without her help."

Carlos closed his com and looked up to find his two young cohorts regarding him with identical expressions.

"What?" he said.

"Not that it's any of my business," Randal began, "but I know Judith will ask. Is there something going on between you and Ava?"

"You're right," Carlos said. "It isn't your business, but yes I do have feelings for her. However, there is nothing but friendship going on between us."

RUN, FOX RUN

AVA SPENT the rest of the afternoon getting her new daughter and guest settled in their rooms.

Tommasa was very surprised at the luxurious quarters she had been given. The bedroom was large enough to encompass an ornately carved desk with a built-in comp and several lounge chairs. It also had an attached bathing room which she would share with Francisca who was next door, and a walk-in closet.

"I hope you like the colors," Aunt Carmen bustled in, followed by Tamara's dressmaker-bot and the lady herself. who seemed to be attempting to ride herd on the older woman.

Carmen opened the closet, which was devoid of clothing. "Bare!" Carmen said with a snort. "Let's see those color swatches, Gelica. We've got to get this girl some clothes!"

Francisca looked at Ava in surprise. "You name your house-bots?"

"Yes. Mother thinks it makes it easier to tell them apart. What can I say? We're a little weird that way."

While the girls were picking out clothing patterns and choosing which materials to feed into the 3-D printer, Carlos, Randal and Devon were on their way home. As soon as they reached the city, Devon and Randal headed for their respective houses. Carlos stopped at his own residence first to clean up before he presented himself at the Garneys.

Although they had been supposed to attend another reception that night,

Agustin vetoed it. "No," he told his wife, "Until we find out who put that viper and the bomb in the carriage, none of us are going anywhere." He fixed his great aunt with a forbidding stare, "That goes for you as well Aunt Carmen."

"Augustin, I've been my own boss for years now," Carmen glared back at him. "I can perfectly well decide for myself what I will or won't do. But as it happens, I agree with you."

"Besides, Mom," Ava interjected, "The girls just got out of the hospital. They need a few days rest before you plunge us all into a round of social visits. Gelicia's good, but they need night clothes as well as other things. She can't possibly get all the clothes run through the 3-D printer in less than 30 minutes! And I want to know if Carlos found the man he went looking for."

When Carlos came by the next morning to bid his daughter goodbye, he found her and Tommasa submerged in clothing patterns and material swaths under the benign supervision of Aunt Carmen, Tash, Judith and Ava.

"It's alright, isn't it Daddy?" Francisca asked. "Aunt Carmen said it was time I had more grown-up clothes. And Tommasa doesn't have any either."

He looked a little dazed at the information unloaded on him. "Who is Aunt Carmen?" he finally asked.

"Well, she's really Tommasa and Ava's aunt but she told me to call her that."

"I'm Carmen," he was told by the elderly woman helping the girls pick out styles.

"Ah—hello," he said. "Certainly, my daughter can have new clothes. Just be sure to send me a bill for it."

"That's very sensible of you, young man," Carmen told him, while Francisca threw her arms around him and kissed his cheek. "I'm glad you agree. Now girls, I think this style will be suitable for learning to fight and shoot."

He looked over at Ava. "She won't help her pick out something outrageous, will she?"

Ava grinned at him. "Probably, but your daughter is growing up. She needs to learn to make her own clothing choices sooner or later."

"Where are you going today?" Agustin asked, shepherding him out of the fitting room.

Carlos cast a hunted look over his shoulder but decided not to interfere with his daughter's choice of new clothes.

"Ah—we planned to take a run down to Dancing Beach. According to the property records Randal and Devon found, Redglove has property down there. It's also where the Housekeeper said his wife was. I'm hoping she will be willing to give us more information about where to find him."

"We expect to be updated after each stage of your hunt," Ava had followed them out of the room. "It makes your daughter anxious if she doesn't know what's going on. That's not fair to her."

Carlos and Agustin both looked unhappy at this. "He might not have time to check in after every movement, Ava," Agustin protested,

"Then he damn well better *find* the time," she retorted, glaring at Carlos.

"I'll try my best; will that do?" he promised.

"I suppose it will have to," she agreed grudgingly.

It was late afternoon when the three sleds crested the hills leading down into the delta. They had followed the Parchester River down its last winding leg to where it met the ocean. The Parchester was fed by many tributary rivers as it made its journey to the sea, and by the time it reached its destination, it was almost 64 KM across.

To one side of the mighty river where it joined the sea, a pristine beach met the shoreline. Drawn by the sight of the Dancing Whisps at morning and evening, it was here that the colonists created one of the main recreation areas on the planet. As befitted a tourist town, the city boasted lots of take-out eateries, sandwich bars and cafés, which offered a plethora of culinary choices. Tourists who weren't hungry enjoyed the beach, water sports, art galleries or one of the many other recreational venues.

"I've got to bring Tash to see this before we go home," Devon vowed. "It's fantastic!"

He was looking at the crowded beach filled with people in various stages of undress, as they played in the waves or sunbathed.

Carlos snorted. "It's quite a scene. Gillian, my first wife and I came here on our honeymoon."

"That was Francisca's mother?" Randal asked.

Carlos nodded. "Yes, I lost her in a sled accident when Francisca was three. She was carrying our second child. We lost him too. And what she would say to me about not protecting our daughter better doesn't bear thinking about."

"How could you know the Red Conclave would order one of their soldiers to kidnap your daughter?" Devon protested.

Carlos sighed. "I should have though; I'd been receiving threats for weeks. I couldn't allow the threats to stop me, but I should have taken precautions to protect my daughter."

"Hindsight is always twenty-twenty," Randal reminded him. "We got her back and now you *can* take those steps."

"Not to change the subject, but Redglove's house is supposed to be in someplace called Carnelian Heights. Any idea where that is?"

"It's this way," Carlos turned his sled, avoiding the traffic crush near the shore and headed down the beach. Several kilometers from the beach play area, the shore turned into A high-end community with magnificent homes, mostly owned by the very affluent. Redglove's home retained the octagon shape set on a plasticrete slab, supported by pilons which could be raised during high water caused by a storm surge coming in off the sea. Like most of the houses in the area, it was surrounded by a tall white wall designed to keep out Barsoom's aggressive flora. Robot gardeners tended the extensive gardens and worked in the houses. supervised by human servants.

Carlos stopped at the gate and pinged the entry buzzer.

Since all three men were tuned to the same wavelength, they saw the smooth face of a robot butler who asked, "How may I help you?"

"I need to speak to Mrs. Redglove," Carlos replied.

"I see. May I ask what this is about?"

"I'll tell her that," Carlos replied, keeping his voice civil. "It's a private matter."

"I see," the robotic voice showed no emotion. "I'm sorry, but Mrs. Redglove had a luncheon engagement in town, and she isn't back yet. If you give me your com information, I will tell her you called."

"Very well," Carlos gave it to him, and turned his sled away. He parked his sled out of sight of the house and got out. Devon and Randal landed and dismounted.

"What do you think?" Randal asked. "Is she there and not receiving visitors, or did she really have a lunch date?"

"My scanner didn't read any trace of human life signs," Devon reported checking his tab.

"Could she have the scanner blocked?" Randal asked.

"After Judith told us it couldn't scan through the basement at the plantation, I up-graded the program. It should go through any blockers," Devon replied.

"There is one more address we can check," Devon offered. "I had the search program running last night and it came up with an address owned by a shell company with ties to Redglove. It's up in the Rainbow Mountains though."

"Let's see it," Carlos said.

The Great Rainbow Range was one of three chains of mountains running in a zig-zag pattern down the spine of Treamamas from the northern edge to the long-tailed south. The ranges didn't connect with each other, being separated by expanses of prairies, valleys and deserts as well as the tropical rain forests near the equator. Neither were they one huge land mass, being broken up by smaller valleys with airable land suitable for farming and ranching.

Devon's topographical map showed Redglove's next safe house was nestled in one of these valleys at the base of a tall basalt mountain. The mountain behind the safe house was covered in a deciduous forest of broadleaf trees, varying in height from very tall to short and scrubby, their growth stinted by lack of sunlight.

It was nearly dark when the posse set their sleds down in a small glen close enough to the safe house to lock into its com system, but too far away to be seen.

"I've got room for all of us to sleep in my sled," Carlos offered. I even have an air mattress for the cargo area. It won't be like home but at least we'll be dry and warm. The sled even has a small microwave."

"Yes, but we need food to cook in it," Devon pointed out.

"Check you saddle bags," Randal suggested. Taking his own advice, he pulled out several packets of the types of pre-packaged meals favored by the Blue Moon Militia on earth.

Devon did the same, and he too found his significant other had stocked his bags with food.

"How did you know this stuff would be there?" he asked.

"I told Judith about the meals we ate that time we stopped at the Militia's safe house. I know she wrote Tash asking if she could bring some of them with you when you came."

"What have you got?" Carlos asked, eyeing the packages.

Sitting cross-legged on the air-mattress, Randal spread out the bounty. "It looks as if she included breakfast, lunch and dinner for at least three days," he said. "With this stuff, we won't even need your cooking toy."

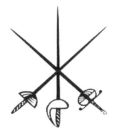

GIRL'S DAY OUT

"HAVE YOU heard from Carlos?" Judith asked, turning off her com. As promised, Randal had updated her about their plans to spend the night in the mountains.

"Yes," Ava said. "He commed to speak to Francisca. Apparently they are going to bc camping out near where he thinks Redglove has gone to ground."

"That was Devon," Tash said. "He said thank you for the MRE's. Since none of them packed any food, I guess they would have gone without if we hadn't taken care of it."

"MREs?" Tommasa asked, "What are those?"

"Meals Ready to Eat," Tash replied. "The Blue Moon Militia stocks them at their safe houses."

"Did they find Redglove's wife?" Tommasa asked.

"No, she was somewhere in town, but they didn't want to try and chase her down. Devon found an address up in the mountains. It's owned by a shell company, but apparently the company has ties to Redglove." Tash sighed. "He mentioned something called the Dancing Whisps, but they didn't see them because they only come out at dawn or dusk to dance on the waves. I'd love to get vid stills of them for my book on colony animals."

"Why not?" Ava said. "Let's plan an overnight trip. We can stay in one of the bed and breakfast places overnight and enjoy the beach a

little during the day. It will keep
me out of Mom's match-making clutches
a day longer."

Judith laughed so hard she cried.

"It's not funny!" Ava protested.
"Do you realize what kind of cretins
she's been dragging out as possible
matches for me?"

"Like that guy at the dinner you
threatened to stab with your knife?"
Judith gasped out.

"You saw that?" Ava asked.

Her sister wiped her eyes, "Yes,
I did. I had all I could do not to
spit out my wine laughing."

"Quite right, too," Aunt Carmen
put in with a grin. "His father and
grandfather were just the same. I've
got an old friend who has a house in
Dancing Beach. Why don't I call her
and ask if she minds if we stay there
overnight?"

"Sounds good to me," Ava said.

Tamara wasn't exactly pleased about the upcoming excursion, but when she learned they planned to stay at a private home, she consented.

Agustin frowned at his great aunt. "I suppose this was your idea?"

"No," Ava said. "It was mine. We'll be staying with one of Aunt Carmen's friends. I think the girls could use a little recreation to help them recover."

"We'll be taking my sled, Agustin," Carmen informed him. "It has stealth mode and weapons; not that I think we'll need them. And Graciella has excellent security at her beach house, because her late husband was paranoid; he was sure an assassin was going to get him."

"Was he right?" Francisca asked, fascinated.

Carmen snorted. "Hell no, he lived to be ninety and died in his sleep."

"That must have been a grave disappointment to him," Ava said with a straight face.

"And you talk about *my* lousy puns," Judith said.

Tommasa giggled. She felt as if she had fallen into a fairy tale. Nothing in her life with the de'Riccis had prepared her for this warm, open family of which she was now a member. The most astonishing thing to her was that they had accepted her so easily.

"Francisca and I both need bathing suits," she reminded Aunt Carmen.

The next morning after breakfast, Tamara and Agustin watched the beach party pile into Carmen's large vehicle.

"Do you think they will be safe?" she asked her husband anxiously.

He threw an arm around her shoulders and hugged her

reassuringly. "From whoever sabotaged our Carriage certainly. Watch."

Just as the tip of Carmen's ancient sled poked it's nose out of the three-tier latticed garage, it wavered and disappeared.

"She's taking no chances; she's invoked the stealth mode. And she wasn't kidding about it being armed. That baby has a built-in pulse cannon."

Ava had elected to sit in one of the rear seats, gladly ceding the shotgun position to Tommasa, who listened avidly as Carmen pointed out the features on the control panel located in the dash.

"Did you tell Randal where we are going?" Ava asked her sister.

Judith shook her head. "His com line was off, but I did leave a text message."

"The same with Devon," Tash said, stroking Fidget's lavender head. The catamount nudged her hand comfortingly.

"Did you com Carlos?" Judith asked her.

Ava nodded, casting a wary eye on Francisca who was sitting beside Tash. "I think they intend to try to get into Redglove's headquarters today."

Judith shivered. "If he gets hurt before our wedding, I'll skin him alive."

"You girls worry too much," Carmen said. "You're all too young to remember; when Carlos Santana was still bounty hunting, he took down a much tougher cartel than the Red Conclave. He brought in their head man then too."

The sled banked sharply to dodge another tree and Ava winced. Their erratic flight path from the city to the Dancing Beach suburbs involved a high-speed weaving in and out between the giant trees who poked their tops out of the rain forest canopy. Carmen was taking no chances on their being caught on vid cam.

Their destination was a house a little outside the city boundary, a graceful, white walled Spanish style with an enclosed patio. The house and grounds were surrounded by a tall, thick brick fence also whitewashed. Carmen brought the sled down near a sleek lattice structure and cut off the stealth mode, so it appeared as if the sled popped out of nowhere.

Carmen's friend, Graciella Cantilupe, was tall and spare, with twinkling blue eyes and silvery hair done up in an elaborate hairstyle. The lines on her tanned face showed she had spent too much time in the sun. She greeted Carmen by throwing her arms around her with a whoop more suited to a teenager than a septuagenarian.

"You came! It's been ages since I've seen you!"

Carmen laughed, grinning back at her. "You must let me introduce you to my family; this is Ava, Judith, Tommasa, Tash, and Francisca."

Graciella smiled warmly at them. "Welcome girls. It will be so nice to have young things about me again. The bots will bring in your luggage. Come and have a nice tall glass of something ice cold."

They spent a carefree afternoon at the city beach, renting boogie boards allowing them to skim along the edge of the water. To no one's surprise, Carmen proved an expert at judging the right time to jump on her board and ride it all the way in. The rest of the party attempted to imitate her skill with varying degrees of success.

Tommasa and Francisca had just dropped their boogie boards off at the rental shop when Tommasa turned around and came face to face with the woman she had called mother for the first fifteen years of her life. Carlotta de'Ricci was, as always, impeccably made up, even for sunning on the beach. The two youngsters with her were ten and eleven. The girl Selina was wearing makeup and looked older than her eleven years—at least thirteen or fourteen. She wore a skimpy thong bikini in imitation of her mother. The boy Alonzo also wore stylish men's trunks, but his mother's influence hadn't kept him from becoming coated with beach sand— probably from building a sandcastle. Tommasa and Mrs. De'Ricci stared at each other in silence for a moment. Later, after she had time to think about it, Tommasa realized the woman was just as shocked and embarrassed as she was. Finally, Tommasa nodded head, "Mrs. de'Ricci," she stepped aside, waiting for Francisca who was flirting with the young man in charge of the board return counter.

Mrs. de'Ricci flushed an ugly shade of red and put protective arms around the boy and girl with her as if she was afraid Tommasa might hurt them. Selina gave her a quick, guilty smile but didn't say anything. Alonzo grinned insouciantly at her, and said, "Hi, sis. When did you get here?"

He's tougher than his sister; Carlotta was going to find it difficult to control him as he got older, Tommasa thought.

Carmen came bustling up. "What's taking you girls so long to return a couple of boards? I'm hungry."

211

Tommasa pointed with her head at Francisca and the boy.

Carmen gave him a once over. "Oh, not bad, but he could use a little seasoning. At least her taste in men is improving. Francisca! You're holding up the line and if we don't check in with the restaurant, they may give away our reservation!"

Reluctantly, Francisca waved goodbye to her new friend and came to join them.

Carmen became aware of the staring contest going on between Tommasa and Mrs. de'Ricci and looked the other woman over suspiciously.

"Introduce me, Tommasa," she prodded.

Tommasa jumped, recalled to reality. "Aunt Carmen, this is Carlotta de'Ricci. She used to be my mother before she disowned me. Mrs. de'Ricci, this is Carmen Garneys, a member of my new family."

Carlotta, whose complexion had almost returned to normal, flushed an ugly red again."

Carmen put a protective arm around Tommasa. "Her loss is our gain," she said. "C'mon girls, we'll miss our reservation."

"Did she really disown you?" Francisca demanded as they walked away.

"She did. Her husband is in politics, and I was an embarrassment. Getting myself kidnapped by the Red Conclave was the last straw for them."

"Gosh!" Francisca said. "I can't imagine Daddy doing that. She sounds like a terrible person."

Tommasa gave a wry laugh. "Honey, you've no idea."

"You're well rid of her," Carmen pronounced. "She had that poor little girl made up like a tart on the Marriage Market!"

Because she had been distracted by her anger at the sight of Selena made up to look like the teenager she wasn't, Carmen, who was usually very attentive to her surroundings, failed to notice the non-descript man watching them from the shade of a nearby tree. Antoni Guissipe had risen high in the Red Conclave ranks because he could so easily fade into the woodwork. He watched them enter the restaurant and concluded they would be there for some time. He went to report to his boss.

Giulio Lupin looked like a body builder. He wore his long, curling blond hair shoulder length. With his looks it had always been easy for him to romance any woman he was directed to.

He had escaped the net spread for the Red Conclave operatives after the hostages at Morthan Castle had been rescued. He hadn't wasted the opportunity to exploit the gap left in the Conclaves ranks by the arrest of so many operatives. His new boss, Adeline Prowd, was second in command next to Jerome Redglove.

"Why are we chasing after a teenage girl, boss?" he asked cautiously. Prowd liked initiative in her operatives, but she would resent it if he seemed to question her decisions. "Not that it matters, but we did some checking into Santana's background last spring when he defended Agustin Garneys, and I discovered he is a dangerous man. Threatening the kid might be the same as poking a stick at an adder."

"I agree, but Elinor Crawley has been helpful in the past. She asked if we could remove the girl, so watch them and if you get the opportunity to take out Francisca Santana or Ava Garneys do it, but don't draw attention to yourself."

Now he looked at Guissipe with a frown. "Well?"

"They went inside the restaurant. I overheard enough to know they plan to stay for the Whisps performance, so they'll be there a while. You want my opinion?"

"Yes, I do."

"We won't get the girl right now. Ava and Carmen Garneys are too aware of their surroundings. If we do it at all it will need to be a sniper."

Lupin considered a moment before he nodded. "Yes, I agree. Waste of time getting rid of the child—I don't know why the Crawley bitch thinks Santana will marry her if his daughter is killed. He's much more likely to marry Garneys. I'm calling this one. We might try again when things cool off."

Nirvana, the restaurant Graciella had chosen was situated almost on the beach. The indoor tables on the terrace were just tall enough to allow patrons a good view of the Whisps when they came out to dance on the waves.

Despite their beach clothes, the headwaiter showed them to their table with every deference.

"Friend of yours?" Carmen asked Graciella with a suggestive wiggle of her eyebrows.

"Yes, but not that kind," her friend responded. "He bats for the other team."

"Pity. With his looks he could make quite a bit of extra income from all the society broads I saw today on the troll. Some of them even seemed to be pimping their daughters."

Tommasa swallowed her iced fruit drink the wrong way and Ava had to pound her on the back. She knew Carmen had been referring to her ex-mother.

"Did you remember to bring your vid-cam?" Judith asked Tash.

Tash lifted a small box with a view-screen she had sat by her plate. "Right here," she said.

They were enjoying a cup of coffee with their deserts when the head waiter announced the appearance of the whisps.

Graciella touched a button on the table, invoking a half circle of silence around it. They could hear each other but not the other patrons,

"Oh," Francisca said softly, "They're beautiful." The Whisps were charming. A soft hum drifted across the waves as they danced gracefully on the crest of them.

"Are they singing?" Tash asked.

"There is some debate over the sounds they make as to whether it's actually an attempt to communicate with us or among themselves," Graciella said softly.

"Are they ever seen at times other than dawn and dusk?" Tash asked.

"They're very shy," Graciella told her. "Occasionally fishermen have spotted a small family group or a single Whisp, but they hide as soon as the fishing boat is spotted."

They were close enough that Tommasa could see their soft, delicate skin which ranged from dark blue, dark grey, purple or light grey or a combination of these colors. Their bodies were semi-transparent, resembling whisps of rainbow hued smoke. Their arms and legs looked like extended strands of smoke. The eyes were dark and almond shaped, and their noses were a small extended bump, their soft lips appeared as a rounded 'O' shape.

The music produced by their dancing grew louder and stronger, and the movements faster and faster before reaching a crescendo. Then, just as suddenly as they had appeared, they were gone, fading into the sunset.

Tash drew a deep breath. "I'm glad I got to see them. Thank you for arranging this Carmen and thank you for allowing us to stay with you Graciella."

Hunting the Bear

CARLOS LAY prone on the hill overlooking Redglove's mountain stronghold. He made a small adjustment on his vid-nocs to pick up noises around his focus area. He hadn't brought any spares with him, but he was unsurprised when Randal and Devon pulled their own out of the side storage panels on their sleds. Probably what Randal had picked up from the Black Templars.

The younger men had taken positions at an angle to his so that they got a slightly different view of the house and grounds.

Redglove hadn't given in to the urge to attract attention by building something fancy—the structure was a simple log cabin although built in the popular octagon shape, with large windows on every side. An extended porch ran around the outside. The grounds had been cleared off to make it difficult to not be seen approaching by any occupants of the house.

'He's got security cams all over the area below us,' Devon texted them. 'It's probably the same surrounding the house.'

'Can you disable them?' Randal texted back.

'I think so, give me a few minutes,' Carlos waited in silence, continually scanning the area.

'Got 'em! I took all of them down, so he won't know where we're coming from.'

Carlos stood up. "Remember," he said through his helmet mic, "This is my fight. Don't interfere unless he has more men hidden inside."

"Of course," Randal agreed, and Devon nodded. Both younger men understood the need for Carlos to personally avenge the attack on his daughter.

Even with the security cams turned off, Carlos knew there was a chance Redglove would spot them when they crossed the cleared area and take a shot at them. He and the two men behind him hugged the trees and bushes surrounding the house.

They took the last few steps to the porch in a rush. Carlos carefully peeked over the floor of the porch, scanning with his com for life signs. He didn't find anyone close, so he stood up and leaped across the porch, coming up hard against the timbered structure. There was a door next to him. He pushed gently and it swung open. As it did so, a pulse bolt screamed through it, crossing the cleared area and hitting a large tree. There was a flash of light as the tree caught fire.

Carlos tucked and rolled in the door, coming up on one knee behind an overstuffed sofa. Redglove's next plasma bolt obliterated the couch, leaving a scorched spot on the hardwood floor. By this time, Carlos had got his foe's direction and he fired back. Redglove was using a commercial grade pistol, which while powerful at close range, was no match for the military style issue Carlos was using.

The powerful bolt of plasma destroyed the door and part of the wall Redglove had been using for cover, but Redglove had already moved on.

It had been several years since Carlos had followed an armed criminal into a structure, but he knew he needed to move after he fired a shot because the other man would aim his weapon at where Carlos had been standing.

Crouching, he made his way into the other room. Redglove had taken refuge in the dining room. There was a crash and the tinkle of broken dishes when he accidentally knocked into a tall Credenza.

Carlos fired a shot in front of the cabinet and heard Redglove cry out. He was still able to run, although he had dropped his pistol. Carlos had clipped him in the shoulder.

Carlos followed the trail of blood, methodically checking each room as he passed. He found Redglove crouched against the far wall.

Carlos could see the blaster burn mark on the porch through the open door. Randal stood about twenty feet away with a raised gun, Apparently Redglove had attempted to run out the door and Randal had fired in front of him to keep him inside the house.

Redglove looked up at Carlos with a snarl of pain. He had been a handsome man: Tall, with even white teeth, his features just avoided being pretty and he was known for his charming smile. His long brown curls were usually carefully styled. Now his hair was a tangled, sweat-streaked mess. His doublet was dirty, and the white shirt he wore under it was torn in several places. In one hand, he clutched his poniard.

Contemptuously, Carlos kicked it out of his hand.

"You're an Officer of The Court Santana," Redglove gasped out, "You can't just kill me."

"You kidnap my little girl and try to turn her into one of your whores, and you think I won't Kill you?" Carlos demanded.

"There are witnesses—" Redglove gasped put. "You'll go to jail—"

He stopped, staring in shock. Randal had mounted the steps to the porch. He was wearing a Black Templar helmet and carrying a helmet with the faceplate covered.

"No," Redglove whispered just before he passed out.

"The Templars would really like to interrogate him," Randal said, waiting for Carlos to decide.

"Why not?" Carlos said. "Just as long as he is disposed of afterwards."

"That can probably be arranged," Randal said, flipping Redglove over on his belly and securing his hands behind him with no regard for the pain it might cause him. To Carlos's surprise, Randal also produced a blacked-out helmet which he put over Redglove's head.

"I've heard about those, but I've never seen one before," Devon said. "It's a blackout helmet isn't it?"

"That's right," Randal agreed. "We don't want him to know where we're taking him or who will be interrogating him."

"How are you going to get him to Templar headquarters?" Devon asked.

"He can ride in the cargo section of my sled," Carlos offered.

As Randal had predicted, Guillaume Peele was delighted with their 'catch'. A tall, slim man with greying hair, he had once been a big name on the stage, and still did a small amount of acting whenever the mood suited him.

"Good job," Mr. Langston, very good. I'll begin the interrogation shortly; will you be staying to watch?"

"Not this time, I'm afraid; we have some anxious ladies waiting for us to return. Perhaps another time?"

"Oh, yes, there will be plenty of opportunities. I imagine the head of the Red Conclave has much to tell us."

He went away whistling a merry tune.

Carlos rolled his eyes. "That's your boss?"

Randal grinned, "He sure is."

YOU ARE MY HEARTBEAT

THE COM CALLS all came in at the same time. Agustin Garneys, who happened to be looking at his eldest daughter, saw her close her eyes in relief when she saw who was calling. Carmen placed a hand on Ava's shoulder and squeezed gently, nodding toward Francisca who was watching Ava anxiously.

"Is that Daddy?" she asked.

Ava smiled at her. "Yes it is. He must have remembered you didn't have a com unit anymore. Come and talk to him."

"Hello Carlos," Ava said. "Did you get him?"

He could see them both, since Ava had an arm around Francisca, who was leaning against her chair.

"Yes, I got him, and none of us are hurt," he added anticipating her next question.

"When are you coming home?" Francisca asked,

"We're on the way now." Carlos told her. "I'm going to stop at the house and clean up before I get there. I stink."

Francisca giggled, and Ava laughed.

"It would be appreciated if our noses didn't announce your arrival before you get here," she said, handing her com to Francisca so she could take a few private moments with her father.

"Excellent," Tamara pronounced. "Tomorrow we can get back to Normal. Just in time for Judith's bridal shower. You can introduce your new daughter to everyone then, Ava."

Tommasa felt a jolt of surprise. The de'Riccis had been more inclined to shut her away when they had guests than introduce her as a member of the family.

"Introduce me?" she whispered to Ava. "I thought—"

"Did you think we were going to hide you in a closet and pretend you don't exist?" her new mother demanded.

"Well, not really, but I didn't expect—"

"Nonsense child," Carmen intervened. "You are a very welcome new member of the Garneys, and we are proud of you."

"Absolutely!" everyone agreed.

Tommasa turned red. "Thank you," she stammered.

"Let's go through your new wardrobe and see what you have

suitable to wear to the bridal shower," Carmen said, putting an arm around her new niece and leading her off.

When Ava would have followed them, her father stopped her. "A moment please Ava," he said.

Ava sank back down in her chair. "Yes?" she asked warily.

"I saw your face just now when we learned Carlos Santana had come through his hunt for Jerome Redglove unscathed. Are you in love with him?"

"I'm not sure but I think I might be," his daughter admitted. "We haven't really had much time to spend together. So much. has been going on— But I have no idea if he feels anything for me but friendship, Dad."

"Time you found out; don't you think?"

Ava smiled wryly. "Probably, but any husband I choose has to be willing to accept Tommasa as well."

"Of course," Agustin agreed." That goes without saying."

"Is that why you've turned away everyone we introduced you to?" her mother demanded. "Why didn't you tell us?"

"Because I don't know how he feels," Ava said. "He has a daughter. I'm sure he won't get married unless she agrees to it. Tommasa needs to agree as well."

"You won't be able to go back to your map charting now that you have a daughter who will be attending school," Tamara said. "Have you thought about what you will do instead?"

"I've got a good-sized nest egg put away. I thought I might finish that book I started writing in high school."

"It will save money if you and Tommasa stay here with us," Agustin suggested.

"That's true, but I've also discussed things with Aunt Carmen. She says she's getting lonely living by herself. She suggested I take her offer to employ me as a paid companion. I would have time to work on my book and she has plenty of room for me and Tommasa."

"I don't like the idea of you isolating yourself to write," her mother protested. "You're young, you need to get out and explore the social scene—"

Ava snorted. "In case it escaped your notice, Aunt Carmen has a very active social life. And I'll have a teenager to chaperone at social events. I won't be bored!"

"And you are much too independent to live with us," Agustin added with a twinkle in his eye.

"Well, yes," Ava admitted.

"Have you told Tommasa about your plans yet?" Tamara asked.

"Yes, we talked about it while we were away. She likes Aunt Carmen."

"I like Aunt Carmen too in small doses," Tamara said dryly. "It isn't the same as living with her."

"We'll manage," Ava said.

She found Carlos and his daughter having a serious discussion in the library. "Am I interrupting something?" she asked.

"Not really," Carlos said. "We were just discussing new rules. Is there something I can do for you?"

"Yes, you can allow Francisca to attend Judith's wedding shower tomorrow. 1 PM, here."

Carlos hesitated. "It's kind of a grown-up affair. Are you sure she will be welcome?"

"Tommasa's coming. I'm sure she would be glad to have someone her age there, and I think a couple of Judith's friends have younger sisters. They'll probably be there as well."

"I have no problem with it. Of course she can come."

"Aunt Carmen is helping Tommasa pick out something appropriate to wear," she told Francisca. "Why don't you join them?"

Francisca jumped up and darted out of the room.

"Do you have a few minutes to talk?" Carlos asked her.

"Of course." She sat down on one of her mother's overstuffed chairs. "Anything in particular you wanted to say?"

"Well, I do want to thank you for taking care of Francisca. She seems like a completely different girl than the one who ran away."

Ava shrugged. "We didn't do much. Just provided her with some new clothes and a trip to see the Dancing Whisps. She's growing up, Carlos. She is about to be pitchforked into her teenage years. It's a difficult time especially for girls. Children learn by imitating the people they are around. She needs some good female role models."

"I know," he said. "I'm hoping you and Tommasa will stay in touch with us. From what she said just now, I can't think of better role models than you and Carmen."

Ava chuckled. "Wait until she starts taking lessons on shooting the pistol and using the poniard Aunt Carmen gave her."

Carlos stared. "A knife? And a pistol?"

"That's right," Ava watched him assimilate this. "Tommasa's going to be taking lessons right along with her."

"I see—that's—do you really think it's necessary?"

"Changing your mind about what type of role models we'll make?"

"No," he said after a moment. "I'm not, Will you have dinner with me tomorrow night?"

"Yes, I'd be delighted to. Formal or casual?"

"There's a French restaurant I thought we'd try."

"Sounds good. What time?"

"Sevenish too early?"

"That's fine. In fact, when you bring Francisca over for the shower, stick in a pair of pajamas and the girls can have a sleepover."

"All right. I guess I'd better collect my daughter from the dress choosing gang."

The girls were delighted with the plans for the sleepover, and immediately began discussing what vid to program to watch.

"A dinner date with Carlos?" Aunt Carmen looked Ava over. "It looks as if you need my assistance in picking out what to wear as well. Casual or Formal?"

"It's that new French Restaurant on the water," Ava said.

"Semi-formal then," Carmen said, examining the clothes in Ava's closet. "None of these will do. Where's that dressmaker bot when you need her? Gelica!" She bustled off to find the bot.

"A date with Carlos, huh?" Tommasa had come to find them.

"That's right," Ava said. "Where's Francisca?"

"Her dad took her shopping for a shower gift. I guess I need to do that too."

Ava made a grimace. "You and me both. I was going to order one delivered. Would you mind doing it that way?"

"I don't have any money," Tommasa reminded her.

"Dad's going to get you set up with a bank account for your allowance as soon as he gets time. In the meantime, I'll put it on my credit chip."

"Okay. What do you give someone for a bridal shower?"

"Lingerie or stuff for the house, towels, dishes, I guess. C'mon, we'll dial it up and see."

While they were waiting for the shopping app to load, Ava took time to bring up the subject of her date.

"Tommasa do you mind my dating Carlos?"

"No, why should I?"

"Because if it goes where I think it's heading, both you and Francisca have a say in what happens. You are now my daughter, and she is his. I need you to think about what it would be like if Carlos and I get married. He will be stepping in as a father to you. As I would be as a mother to Francisca, so both of you need to be willing for it to happen. Just give it some thought,"

"Alright."

Carlos and his daughter had nearly the same discussion until he mentioned he might marry Ava.

"I like Ava," Francisca said, "You should have seen her flip the Wicked Witch of The West on her butt when she tried to hit me. Just like a real mom would."

"Some woman tried to hit you? When? Who was it?"

"At the hospital. She said I was a little bitch and tried to slap me. Ava got between us and flipped her over on her butt. It was great."

"*Who was it?*"

"Elinor Crawley. She tried to say she was going to marry you and you were going to send me off to boarding school to get rid of me. I said it was a lie and she tried to slap me."

"Don't worry about her. She'll never get near you again."

"Aunt Carmen said it's important for girls to learn to protect themselves. That's why she got me the pistol and the knife. As soon as I learn to use it, I'm going to start wearing them the way Aunt Carmen said to."

Carlos closed his eyes briefly, wondering if he should have second thoughts about the kind of role models Ava and Carmen Garneys would make. Well, he wanted Ava, so he realized he was going to need to accept them as they were. Francisca would undoubtedly come out of their tutelage a much stronger woman.

BATTLE LINES

CARLOTTA DE'RICCI wasn't pleased at the way the Garneys were introducing Tommasa to everyone. They made no secret of the fact the de'Riccis had virtually disowned the girl. It was beginning to be embarrassing. So, she decided to do something about it.

She managed to get an invitation to the next wedding celebration given for Judith and Randal. It took a little bit of doing, but when she saw Tommasa go into the library for a few minutes respite from the dancing, she followed her.

"Doing all right for yourself, I see," she said.

Tommasa looked up warily. "What do you want?"

"Is that any way to speak to your mother?"

"You aren't my mother. You're my aunt."

"You're a bastard conceived in a rape. You're lucky we housed and fed you for fifteen years. We should have turned you over to social services when you were born." Carlotta retorted. "Your mother didn't even know who your father was."

"Yes, I already know that." Tommasa said wearily. "I repeat, what do you want?"

"I want you to go away and stay away." Carlotta hissed.

"Why should I?" Tommasa demanded. "I have a real family now. Why should I leave?"

"A real family?" Carlotta sneered. "How much do you think that 'real' family will want you around when I tell everyone, Agustin Garneys is your father? That he raped your mother?"

"That's a lie! He wouldn't do a thing like that!" Tommasa cried.

Carlotta laughed. "It doesn't matter if he's innocent of the charge or not. People love that kind of gossip!"

She turned and left. "I'll give you three days." She said over her shoulder.

Tommasa held it together until the woman was gone, then she collapsed on the chair in tears. The thought the people who had given her such a warm welcome might come to despise her was heartbreaking.

Ava found her like that when she came in search of her. "I just saw that bitch Carlotta de'Ricci leave—what's wrong? What did she say to you?"

Tommasa shook her head, "It's nothing—"

"Bullshit!" Her new mother said roundly. "If you won't tell me, I'll hunt her down and make *her* tell me."

Tommasa sat up and wiped her eyes with her fingers.

"Here, wipe and blow." Ava handed her a box of tissues.

After she blew her nose, Tommasa said, "If I don't leave, she's going to tell everyone your father raped my mother and that I'm his bastard. Your mother will hate me—"

"No, she won't" Ava said. "When she finds out that bitch is threatening you, she'll eat her alive."

"What?" Tommasa said.

"You heard me. Will you wait here while I go get her?"

"I—yes. I'll wait."

"What are you girls doing, hiding out in here?" Carman demanded, coming into the room. "There's a party going on out there. You're missing it."

"Just the person I wanted to see. Carlotta de'Ricci has been threatening Tommasa. She'll tell you about it while I go and get Mom."

Carmen sat down in a chair. "What did she say child?"

Ava found her mother fussing with Judith's hair, which had come down because of a romantic encounter with her fiancé.

"Mom, Tommasa and I need you in the library. Its an emergency."

Tamara looked up sharply. "There, that should do it. Tell that boy not to make a mess of your hair the next time he kisses you."

"What's going on Ava?"

"That bitch Carlotta de'Ricci just threatened Tommasa."

"Threatened her? Why?"

Ava grinned nastily. "Because we aren't hiding her in a closet as if we were ashamed of her. Wait until you hear what she threatened her with."

When she and Ava arrived in the library, they found Carmen still there. The older woman was seething.

"It's about time you got here," she told Tamara. "Do you know what that de'Ricci bitch has threatened to do?"

"No," Tamara said, her eyes narrowing, "Tell me."

"Yes, tell us," Judith had followed her mother and Ava.

Tommasa took a deep breath. "She said if I don't disappear she is going to tell everyone Agustin raped my mother and I'm his bastard. Please don't hate me."

Tamara put both arms around the distraught girl. "Don't be silly child. How could I hate you? I already love you. You quit worrying about her and what she might say. Leave her to me. I'll settle her hash."

Behind her back, Ava winked at Tommasa.

"To us," Carmen seconded.

"Let's go find her," Tamara said.

The older women left the room, a pair united in battle.

"See? What did I tell you? Want to go and watch?"

"I do," Judith said, following her mother and Carmen.

Tommasa's spine straightened. "Yes," she said firmly. "So do I."

That's my girl," Ava said.

Tamara and Carmen found Carlotta about to take her leave of her hostess, well satisfied with the completion of her plans. In three days, unless she was mistaken,

Tommasa would only be a blip on the Garneys radar.

"Carlotta de'Ricci!" Tamara's voice rang like a bell. Several people turned to look.

"Yes?" Carlotta answered warily, perhaps she had misjudged the little bitch after all. She must have run straight to Tamara with the threat.

"I hear you have something to tell me about my husband and my Granddaughter?" Tamara made no effort to lower her voice and more people turned to stare.

"About my Great-nephew and my niece?" Carmen too didn't lower her voice. She had been an actress before she retired, and her voice filled the room as it had once filled theatres. By this time just about everyone was avidly watching the quintette at the door.

When Ava, Tommasa and Judith appeared behind Carmen and Tamara,

Carlotta swallowed visibly. Ava and Judith had Tommasa sandwiched protectively between them. It was a clear statement Tommasa was now family and that meant they would protect her. It was time to retreat and regroup; providing the Garneys would let her.

"Well?" Tamara demanded.

"I don't know what you heard." Carlotta said, "but I don't have anything to tell you."

"You'd better not," Tamara said, her eyes flat and cold. "Because if I hear even a whisper of this, I won't confront the whisperer; I'm coming to see you. I'll be very angry. And you won't like me when I'm angry. You understand me?"

Carlotta stared back at her with compressed lips. The two women locked eyes.

"I didn't hear you," Tamara said. "Do you understand? Let me hear you say it."

"I understand," Carlotta said finally, realizing Tamara meant business.

She bid her hostess goodbye and left.

Tamara turned to her hostess, an apology on her lips, only to find Geraldine laughing like a hyena. She waved off Tamara's apology, "You just ensured my party will be the social event of the year."

Carlotta wasn't the only woman who wanted a child to disappear. Elinor suddenly found her attempts to reach Carlos weren't going through. His office simply told her he was 'unavailable', and the robot butler who controlled his home, refused to allow her to come in and leave a message for him.

Furious, she commed her friend with connections. "Francisca has to go," she told Adeline Prowd. "Obviously, kidnapping her didn't make a difference, and he got her back anyway."

"I'm sorry, but I've helped you all I can," Adeline said, "I could justify using Conclave time and resources when there was hope holding the daughter might make Santana back off prosecuting our people. With Redglove now in custody, I can't afford to waste resources that way."

"What about a using a sniper to kill her?" Elinor asked.

"I can give you a name, and his contact information, but you'll have to pay his fee yourself. He doesn't come cheap."

"How much is he likely to cost me?"

Adeline told her.

"That's a lot of credit," Elinor said.

"I warned you. Do you still want his information?"

"Yes, give it to me."

Tobias Tudor looked Elinor over in silence. Elinor judged him to be about forty, with hard eyes in a wrinkled face. None of his clients had ever realized he'd had adaptive surgery early in his career to increase his eyesight; neither did Elinor, nor would she have cared.

"If you hadn't given me Adeline's name, I would turn you down."

"*Are* you going to turn me down?" she asked,

"Depends. Who is the hit on?"

"Carlos Santana has a daughter, here is a vid still of her. The 'hit' as you call it, is on her. Carlos is not to be harmed."

"You want to take out his kid rather than Santana?"

"Yes. Will you do it?"

"I charge extra for kids. Have the credits put in this account by 5'Oclock today. I don't act until the deposit is made."

"It will be there."

The credit showed up in the designated account, so three days before the wedding, Carmen arrived after lunch to pick up Francisca for her first shooting lesson. Carmen was dressed in body fitting armor and she had Tommasa already in the sled.

Many sleds on Barsoom were shaped like falcons or other birds of prey. Carmen had to be different; her sled was reminiscent of a large water bird. It was long, sleek, and bright pink with a darker nosecone which hooked downward. Carlos hadn't seen it the last time she had flown the girls anywhere. He stood gaping at it for a moment. "Your sled design is—quite remarkable," he said.

Carmen grinned at him. "Yes, it is, isn't it."

"What time can I expect her back?" Carlos asked.

"Sometime late this afternoon."

"I need to go into the office for a few hours. Perhaps you could take Francisca back to the Garneys when you get done and I'll pick her up when I get through?"

Carmen smiled approvingly at him. "And maybe see Ava while you're at it?"

"Yes," he said with a smile.

"Bye Daddy," Francisca headed for the sled.

Just as she opened the door a pulse bullet ricocheted off Carmen's armor, knocking the older woman into Francisca.

"Get in the sled!" Carlos roared, firing his pistol at where the shot came from.

Tommasa leaned out of the door and pulled Carmen inside, hitting the stealth control as she did so. Francisca had scrambled inside and turned to help drag the elderly woman into the sled.

Carlos helped lift Carmen, Scooting the older woman over on the seat so he could close the door as he too climbed inside.

"It's a good thing I wore armor today," Carmen puffed when she could get her breath back. "Stop fussing girls! I'm okay."

"You are not okay," Tommasa countered. "The shot might not have penetrated the armor, but I bet it's going to leave one Hell of a bruise."

Satisfied they weren't visible, Carlos started the sled and headed for a nearby urgent care clinic. "We'll get you checked out anyway," he said.

Carmen sat up. "Now see here young man, I've been taking care of myself for more years than you can count. I'll tell you when I need to see a doctor—are you listening to me?"

"No," Carlos replied. He tagged Agustin on his com and after explaining what happened, he arranged to meet him at the clinic.

"Please, Aunt Carmen." Tommasa said.

"We need to know you are okay," Francisca chimed in, tears in her voice.

Carmen eyed both girls malevoently. "You can knock off the tears," she informed Francisca. "I was a great actress, I know when I'm being railroaded, young lady."

Francisca grinned at her unrepentedly. "Well, it was worth a try."

Carmen snorted out a laugh, then winced. "Kid don't make me laugh—that bruise Tommasa talked about is right over my laugh muscles."

THE 12ᵀᴴ OF NEVER

BARSOOMIAN COLONISTS loved the Renaissance. However, they tended to pick and choose which customs to imitate when setting up their new colony. They wanted to keep the 'romance' of the culture without stepping back technologically or getting bogged down in time wasting customs such as the day long church service accompanying Renaissance weddings.

Randal spent the evening before his wedding at a bachelor party thrown by Devon and Ailwin. Carlos was invited, but he declined the invitation in favor of a family dinner with only himself, Ava and their two daughters at the new French restaurant, les Amis Elementaire.

Francisca eyed the menu suspiciously. "Dad what is Escargot?"

"Don't try it," Tommasa advised. "It's snails. I watched the cook at the De'Riccis prepare it once. Yuck."

"What are you going to have?" Francisca challenged.

"Soupe a L'oignon followed by The Ratatouille; it's a kind of stir-fried stew. No snails."

"Ava?" Carlos asked.

"The Beouf Bourguingnon with Lyonnaise potatoes, I think."

"That sounds excellent," Carlos said. He gave the order to the waiter, adding, "Ava and I will share a bottle of your best Burgundy. The young ladies are allowed one glass, then switch them to Iced Tea."

"Is this what it will be like if you two get married?" Francisca asked.

"Well, we won't be going out to dinner every night," Ava said. "I expect the family will eat most meals in. However, I'm sure the Chef-bot can be programed with some French recipes."

"But not snails, please," Tommasa shuddered.

Ava chuckled, "I don't like them either," she agreed.

The conversation might have segued into a discussion of culinary likes and dislikes, but Francisca had an agenda which she wasn't to be diverted from.

"That means Daddy will be home for it, doesn't it? No more working overtime," she said with satisfaction.

All of them looked at Carlos. He realized he was trapped. "I will do my best to be home in the evenings."

"No," his daughter said. "You have to *promise* to be there."

"Do my best *is* a trifle vague," Ava pointed out.

He met her eyes ruefully. "Very well, I promise to be home in the evenings. Will that do?"

"Yes, I think so, don't you girls?" Ava asked.

"You're awesome at the negotiating table," Tommasa told Francisca, who grinned back at her.

Carlos cleared his throat. "I realize this is quite sudden," he said, getting up from his chair and coming to get down on one knee in front of Ava, who had swiveled her chair to face him when she realized he was coming around to face her.

Carlos produced an ornately carved small box and held it out to her. "Ava, will you and Tommasa marry us?"

It took a lot to throw Ava, but she felt her face heat up, she glanced over at Tommasa, who nodded energetically

"Yes," she stammered. "I will be honored to be your wife."

The box contained a Firey emerald sandwiched between two brilliant stones, one blue and one yellow.

"It's beautiful, Carlos." She said, holding it up for the girls to see.

"I got your ring size from your mother," Carlos said, taking it from her and slipping it on her finger. He kissed her hand and got up from the floor.

The waitstaff at les Amis Elementaire prided themselves on keeping an eye on their customers. At a signal from the Concierge, the waiter brought over a chilled bottle of sparkling wine.

When Carlos and Francisca took them home, Francisca stayed in the sled while he walked Ava and Tommasa to the door. Ava unlocked it, and he took Tommasa by the shoulders and ushered her inside, closing the door behind her, saying "Inside, brat, Ava and I want a little privacy."

When he kissed her, the kiss began gently, but when she wrapped her arms around his neck, it quickly changed to passionate and demanding.

"Goodnight," when he raised his head, his voice was a little thick.

"Goodnight," her own voice was breathless.

"When she went inside, she found her family waiting expectantly.

"Big mouth," she told Tommasa

"I told them," Tommasa said, grinning.

"Let's see the ring," Judith and Aunt Carmen demanded.

The bachelor party lasted a lot longer than the family dinner. About one in the morning, Devon found Randal making a pot of coffee.

"Not drinking?" Devon asked Randal, who had switched from the highly spiced alcoholic Mead being served most of the guests, to coffee.

"I'd rather not be hung over at my wedding," Randal replied.

"I thought the drunken bridegroom was the custom at Renaissance weddings." Devon remarked grinning.

Randal shrugged. "Sometimes it is, but it's not essential. We kind of pick and choose which customs we practice."

"Really?" Devon was interested." Which ones did you keep? Besides Code Duello, I mean."

"Well, we are skipping the one about spending the day in church hearing mass. We do say our vows on the church steps, then the guests follow us back to a fourteen-course banquet. We'll be opening gifts in between some courses and watching some mimes and tumblers exhibit their skill. There will also be dancing. The entire affair takes about five hours."

"Wow!" Devon said, taking a swallow of his tea. "Remind me not to agree if Tash takes a notion for a Renaissance ceremony when *we* get married."

"Planning that any time soon?"

"Tash's sister Joyce is planning it. Probably going to take place during the Spring Equinox Festival in Laughing Mountain."

One of the wedding customs kept by the colonists was the gathering of special women guests to dress at the bride's home, so they could admire her dress and each other's.

Carlos managed a few words with Ava when he dropped Francisca off to dress with the rest of the family.

"How soon do you think we'll be doing this?" he asked.

"In a hurry?" Ava asked archly.

"Yes," he admitted ruefully.

"Give Mom time to catch her breath," Ava said, giving him a kiss. "I doubt if it will be very long—she's been itching to marry me off for years." She said with a chuckle.

Judith's wedding dress was a light cream, trimmed in gold, with a square, low-cut neckline. An attached hood which could be lifted in case it rained during the outdoor ceremony draped over her shoulders. The sleeves were tight to the elbow with gold braid circling her upper arms. Long, loose chiffon sleeves descended to cover her hands. The waist was cinched under her breasts with gold ribbon, to show off her Rubenesque figure.

The guests wore Renaissance gowns of the same style, most of them in vibrant shades of blue, green, yellow and red trimmed in contrasting shades of color. Many of the gowns had a slit for easy reach of a poniard sheath on a woman's thigh.

For Tommasa and Francisca, this was the first time either of them had worn such an elaborate gown.

Aunt Carmen busied herself teaching the girls how to reach the weapon, and how to move in the long dresses so their legs wouldn't get tangled in it and trip them up.

"Very good, Francisca," she said. "Now you try it Tommasa."

On her mettle to get it right the first time, Tommasa reached into the slit and drew the knife, at the same time aiming a kick at an imaginary opponent.

"Good," Carmen praised. "Now remember girls, never draw the knife without being willing to use it."

"I'd be willing," Tommasa said. "I just wish I'd had it when Redglove's men grabbed me."

Instead of a walking procession to the church, the wedding party were ferried there in gondolas. The robot gondoliers sang a selection of Renaissance wedding songs, Frescobaldi's Bergamasca, Dulcissime and Rondeau to accompany the water procession.

As befitting the bride's family, Ava and the others gathered at the base of the church steps to hear and see the marriage vows.

It was a lovely ceremony, Judith and Randal stared dreamily into each other's eyes as they said their vows.

For them, no one else existed at that moment.

Ava met Carlos's eyes and smiled. Just over his shoulder, she caught the glint of metal on a plasma bolt rifle.

"Down! Get down! He's got a gun!" she yelled, dragging the two girls down with her. Everyone in the crowd, including Judith and Randal hit the ground as the plasma bolt sizzled by overhead. Carlos, Agustin, Timothy Langston and several others drew pistols and fired at the area the shot came from.

"Keep them down!" Carlos ordered, crouching in front of Ava and the girls to protect them as he returned fire. Ava caught a glimpse of the body armor he wore under his celebration clothes. Obviously he was taking no chances the Red Conclave might retaliate after his capture of

Redglove; otherwise, why had he worn body armor and a pistol to a wedding?

The bevy of shots aimed at the sniper's former position blew a hole in a building across from the church.

Unlike the others, Carlos had been expecting the sniper to move; his shots were aimed at both sides of Tudor's position forcing the sniper to run.

The client had said Santana was not to be harmed; that might not be possible. Tudor had accepted money for the assassination, despite the earlier failed attempt, he had to keep trying.

One of the shots hit Tobias; his personal shield bubble was efficient if he wasn't moving; it was less so if he needed to run, and it slowed him down. Even though no pulse bullets could penetrate it, the surface of the shield didn't absorb the kinetic energy it generated. To block the penetrating force of the bullet, the shield would harden and thicken where a shot hit it. Being hit by a great many at once meant the hardened area increased in size and weight. Although the last shot didn't penetrate his shield, it numbed his hands, and he dropped the rifle. It clattered to the building dock below him before bouncing into the water. He swore as the guests centered their fire where the rifle would have fallen from.

Repeated pulse hits on the shield knocked him off his perch on the building, and he too fell. He hit the deck hard, knocking himself out when his head smacked his shield as he hit the ground.

Timothy Langston and Agustin ran over to the fallen sniper.

"Take the girls back to the house and stay there with them," Carlos

275

ordered before he went to join the two fathers.

"Randal, I might have known you couldn't get married without something like this happening," Devon groused, levering himself up from the plasticrete deck and holding out a hand to assist Tash, who was hampered by her long skirts.

"Who do you think it is?" Tash asked brushing at her crumpled skirt.

"A hired gun, probably," Ava said. She snagged Francisca's hand when the girl would have followed her father. "No, stay here, Francisca. You heard your father say to wait for him back at the house."

"If we weren't here, would you obey that order?" Francisca challenged.

Ava sighed. Being a parent was hard. She wanted to go and get in on the action as much as Francisca did.

"You are here, so it's a moot point young lady. Stay with me."

Francisca's lip trembled. "What if he hurts him?"

"Don't waste that on me, kid. I'm not an actress like Aunt Carmen but I can tell when tears are real just well as she can."

"Dammit!" Francisca stamped her foot. Tommasa patted her on the shoulder in consolation.

Aunt Carmen had summoned her Flamingo pink sled. She herded her family and Randal's into it.

Randal deposited his bride at the sled door, telling Judith he would come as soon as he found out what was going on.

They managed to beat most of the wedding guests to the banquet hall the Langston's had rented for the reception.

"I bet I'm the only bride in history who had an uninvited sniper crash the wedding and then had to celebrate her bridal feast without the groom!" Judith said acidly as she sat down.

"At least they caught him." Carmen said. "If Ava's right though, and he's just a hired gun he might not tell them who hired him."

"It has to be someone from the Red Conclave," Tamara said. "Who else could it be?"

"I thought that broke up when Carlos killed the leader," Allison Langston protested.

Tamara made a face. "Agustin told me the thing was like a hydra—cut off a head and two more would grow in its place. Maybe the new leader is flexing his power by trying to kill the man who killed their leader?"

"Daddy!" Francisca gasped in fright.

"Shut up Mom," Ava said gesturing to the girl's white face.

"Your dad was wearing body armor, Francisca, he should be okay," she said, giving the girl a comforting hug. Francisca turned her face into Ava and burst into frightened tears. Ava patted her soothingly, glaring at the group.

Since none of them wanted to scare the child, they all looked embarrassed and contrite. Judith signaled the performers to start, hoping to take Francisca's mind off her fear for her father. She was only partially successful; Francisca tensed every time a door opened.

The entertainers were doing a lively skit on the perils of marriage when the men arrived back.

Carlos came over to his new family. "We caught him, but he refused to talk."

"Does that mean someone else will try again?" Ava asked, she was holding hands with the two girls, and she felt both girls tense when she asked the question.

"It's always possible," Carlos said, "But from a few things he said under the influence of the Black Templar's interrogation drugs, I think whoever hired him was acting on his or her own."

"Her?" Ava asked. "Do you think it was his wife?"

"I don't know," Carlos admitted, "He had a poison tooth—when he realized he was talking under the drug's influence, he broke it. He's dead. We'll just have to be careful. The Conclave was already gunning for me before I took out Redglove."

"Okay," Francisca agreed.

"We need more lessons from Aunt Carmen," Tommasa said.

"Yes," Francisca agreed.

THE COLONY OF BARSOOM*

HISTORY

Barsoom was a Planned Colony. The Barsoomians petitioned Earth-Gov to open a new colony along with several other organizations. However, upon discovering Earth-Gov insisted all its new colonies adopt the same laws and regulations as those governing post-apocalyptic Earth, they withdrew their application. The new colonies under Earth-Gov's auspices were not given the right to govern themselves nor did they have a vote when those laws were made. Barsoom, like Arcadia, decided NOT to become an Earth-Gov protectorate and instead petitioned Laughing Mountain to find them a suitable planet to colonize which they could run by *their* rules.

What if the d'Medici's and Borgias, or artists such as *Raffaello (Raphael) Sanzio da Urbino and Michelangelo, or scientists like Copernicus and Galileo had possessed advanced technology?*

The Outlawed Colony of Barsoom* was designed to be a mix of renaissance dress and manners coupled with advanced technology. By day, the colonists invented nanites to cure diseases and cast illusions. By night, they caroused in taverns and ballrooms served by robots. At dawn, they fought duels over imagined or real insults.

The new planet the colonists christened Barsoom* (I received authorization to use the name from ERB, Inc. providing I give credit for the trademark to them in each novel) has the requisite two moons, but it has a tropical climate. Since their main industry is the manufacture of micro robots, stringent steps are taken to prevent the deterioration of the robots.

Socially, Barsoom* enjoys a renaissance lifestyle. It was colonized by groups of people who wanted to keep the romance of a renaissance culture but retain their technology. Colony organizers spent months sending through anything they thought they might need. Barsoom's Education level is high. The main industries are research and creating tiny robots called nanites which can be programmed for various medical, scientific instruments and weapons. Farming, fishing, merchants, and mining are also part of the colonies economic base, but since they love their high-tech gadgets, much of the manual labor in these industries is done by robots. The colonists also import many small circuits to make their metal servants with.

Since Barsoom employs Robots for many manual tasks, it doesn't have a 'noble' class system, but instead utilizes a more modern egalitarian way of classifying it's population.

GENERAL

DESCRIPTION

The Planet itself is well within earth normal standards as far as temperature. It has two moons who orbit close together. Their combined mass is approximately 1½ the size of

Earth's moon. The planet has nine continents, the majority of which are scattered along the equator, with 68% of the planet water. The salty ocean waters were warm thanks to the tropical current circling between the next largest land mass (dubbed Mayone) and Treamamas, the continent where the Portal was located. Treamamas, the largest continent is Kite shaped. About 1/3 of it is in the northern temperate zone and the rest of it descends with its narrow tail in the southern temperate zone. The largest land mass in the tropics.

Although most of the colonists decided to settle near the portal which is in the tropics, the planet has enough arable land for farming. The colonists are still engaged in mapping the new world and discovering new animal species, most of which seem to be compatible genetically enough with humans to provide food sources if need be.

Although they have topographical maps of the planet, Colonists are only actively engaged in exploring Treamamas. The other eight continents from largest to smallest, are Mayone, Iablari, Sashoa, Troyai, Ridall, Tresoni, Kritual, and Luasilith. Plans for exploring them exist, but not in the immediate future.

It takes 425 days to orbit the sun, and each day is 27 hours. The colonists use the Greek Calendar in naming the months, with each month being between 33 and 38 days.

- Januarius (January)   38
- Februarius (February)   33
- Martius (March)   36
- Aprilis (April)   36
- Maius (May)   36
- Iunius (June)   36
- Quintilis (July)   38

- Sextilis (August)   36
- September (September)   36
- October (October)   36
- November (November)   36
- December (December)   38
- **Total to make a year**   **435**

The Portal came out close to the equator. The capital city of Savano where the Portal is located, has been built to withstand the predations of tropical, fast-growing plants, and extreme humidity (it rains nearly every day). The colony is troubled by insects so they Cultivate the Lint Dragons and Hermit Flyers to assist with bug control. Farmlands have been cleared and the soil is fertile, but the crops are under constant attack by native plants. Most of the cultivating is done by robots.

GEOGRAPHICAL FEATURES

GREAT RAINBOW MOUNTAINS

These mountains are part of three chains of mountains running in a zig-zag pattern down the spine of Treamamas (the continent where the Terrans settled) from the northern edge to the long-tailed south. The ranges do not run in a straight line, being separated by expanses of prairies, valleys and deserts as well as tropical rain forests near the equator. Neither are they one huge mass, being broken up by smaller valleys with airable land suitable for farming and ranching. The other two ranges were named Gildover Range, and Chibougamau Mountains, both largely unmapped, except for topographical images.

PARCHESTER RIVER

It is a long, winding river, one of the main rivers on Barsoom and is fed by many small tributaries, growing deeper and wider as it extends towards the sea. The headwaters are somewhere in the Great Rainbow Mountains, so called because of the iridescent sheen reflected during certain times of the year. The delta estuary where the river meets the Langstino Sea is marked by pristine beaches which are much enjoyed by Barsoom's populace. The river is approximately 64Km wide and filled with hundreds of small islets created by the silt carried downriver during storms.

LANGSTINO SEA

Although the Barsoomian colonists had chosen to keep the Off-World Portal in the tropic zone where Laughing Mountain's scientists had first made the connection, extensive drone mapping had also taken place. Thus, the colonists had a working topographical map of the planet; they had located all the major land masses, rivers, mountains and deserts in the initial survey. They had also made sure no sentient life already occupied the planet. The ocean to the southeast of the portal had been dubbed the Langstino Sea, after the first woman who mapped the area. The salty waters were warm thanks to the tropical current circling between the next largest land mass (dubbed Mayone) and Treamamas, the continent where the main settlement was located.

SOCIAL VALUES AND MANNERS

- A native of Barsoom should possess the qualities of good character, grace, and talents.
- A native of Barsoom should be learned and should practice

291

certain physical and military exercises.

- A native of Barsoom should have a classical education and should be able to play and instrument or be a proficient artist.

As mentioned before, Barsoom allows dueling. This is a highly stylized and organized method of settling individual disputes.

CODE DUELLO

Code Duello is a set of rules for a one-on-one combat, or **duel**. Code duello regulates dueling and thus helps prevent **vendettas** between families and other social factions. The code ensures a non-violent means of reaching an agreement and that harm be reduced, both by limiting the terms of engagement and by providing medical care. Finally, Code Duello ensures that the proceedings have several witnesses and a judge. The witnesses are there to assure grieving members of factions of the fairness of the duel and provide testimony if legal authorities become involved.

A morally acceptable duel would start with the challenger issuing a traditional, public, personal grievance, based on an insult, directly to the single person who offended the challenger.

The challenged person had the choice of a public apology, other restitution or choosing the weapons for the duel. The challenger would then propose a place for the "field of honor". In the Capital city of Barsoom a field has been designated specifically for dueling. For a duel to be legal, participants must use this location which provides a judge to decide if the duel has been fair.

The Dueling field also has rotating doctors on call to attend each duel.

Each side would have at least one second; two was the traditional number.

If one party failed to appear, he was considered a coward, and the appearing party would win by default. The seconds (and sometimes the doctor) would bear witness to the cowardice. The resulting reputation for cowardice would often considerably affect the individual's standing in society, perhaps even extending to their family also.

The opponents agreed to duel to an agreed condition, either First Blood, Death or until either party was no longer able to fight, or the physician called a halt.

When the condition was achieved, the matter was considered settled with the winner proving his point and the loser keeping his reputation for courage.

∧∩I∧∧LS

FYI: some of the animal illustrations were created using Artificial Intelligence technology derived from written descriptions from the author.

LINT DRAGON: A small, warm blooded, four-legged winged mammal. It is covered in very fine fur and

resembles a floating ball of rainbow-colored lint. It is omnivorous with a diet consisting of berries, nuts, small insects, and grubs. Normally found in family groups consisting of several females and males of various ages and ranks and their fledglings. One dominant pair rules the others. Some family groups will band with others to form a herd with one supreme pair who rules. Because of their small size (about the size of a hamster) they have very few offensive weapons, but they do possess a painful sting. When a flock acts in unison to drive off a predator, their combined sting can cause injury or even death depending on the size of the predator. They can form a flock bond with a human, but only if they are socialized when they are very young. Mostly they are used domestically to help control Barsoom's burgeoning insect population.

CATAMOUNT: a small native mammal adopted by colonists as pets. It's

about the size of a Guinea pig. It looks hairless, but the hair is so fine it's transparent. It has large, bat-like ears, big eyes which change in the dark. It is Omnivorous with a diet of fish, crustations, berries nuts and occasional insects. Catamounts Like water, and in the wild can be seen swimming in shallow water. They are usually found singly or in small family groups. Adolescents move on when they reach maturity. Despite their small size, they Can be fierce in defense of their clan.

HAIRY CATAMOUNT: This variety has a short, dense coat of golden fur fading to white around the paws and

face. The loose skin under the dense fur is wrinkled, probably a defense against being grabbed by a predator. Like their hairless relatives they are

Omnivorous with a diet of fish, crustations, berries nuts and occasional insects. They are usually found singly or in small family groups.

KEVLAR: Kevlars are a Medium to large carnivore, with shaggy, green mottled fur, pointed ears and eyes on

the side of the head. They run in packs. Although they do have some feline characteristics, The xenozoologists say they fill the same niche on Barsoom as wolves did on earth. They also have a similar pack social structure.

GREYHOUND DEER

A small ruminant living in the broadleaf forests. It has a Dainty

body like that of a greyhound dog, sharp, pointed antlers, thin legs. Herds are most often found in the small meadows where they can quickly take shelter in the forest. Their meat is considered a delicacy, and the colonists hunt them with bow and arrow or crossbows. Using any other weapon is considered dishonorable.

HERMIT FLYER

This animal has a vivid yellow, scaly hide and a body shaped like a hamster. Its face resembles that of  a cat and its eyes remind you of a mouse's. It has large round ears and a pair of feathery wings. It weighs About 12 lbs. It is a mammal, not a bird, but it is found in family groups like birds. They roost in trees in the wild. It is an Omnivore whose main diet is insects and grubs, but they will eat vegetation if that is all that is available. Like the Lint Dragons, they were domesticated by the colonists for use in helping control Barsoom's flourishing insect population.

ᴡᴴɪꜱᴘꜱ:

They are a type of aquatic mammal. They have a soft, delicate skin which

is usually either dark blue, dark grey, purple or light grey or a combination of these colors. Their bodies are semi-transparent, resembling whisps of rainbow smoke. They have arms and legs which look like extended whisps of smoke. Upon close inspection, their faces have dark eyes, a small nub where the nose should be and soft lips forming and O when they hum (or sing). They dance upon the tops of the waves in the dawn and at dusk during high tides.

PLANTS

All flora on this world is aggressive. It is fast growing and will quickly take over a field of crops if not kept under quick control. This is mostly done with robots, although the Barsoomians are very interested in genetically altering plant species imported from earth to be strong enough to hold their own with native flora.

Although the vegetation surrounding the portal and other cities in the tropical reason resembles a tropical rainforest, other areas of the planet enjoy a normal range of deciduous forests in the upper elevations and long grasses in the temperate regions.

COLONIAL SETTLEMENTS

CAPITAL CITY: SAVONA

Savona sits near the edge of a shallow lake. The buildings, like the houses are Octagon shaped, with rainwater and solar collectors. The city was designed by a man who was greatly enamored of Venice, Italy. However, he had radical ideas as to how to avoid the issues with flooding and sinking that besets that city on earth. He designed the capital city buildings as a series of floating platforms, like the design used on aircraft carriers on old earth. Each building was on a separate platform, and connected below the water with force field magnets which allowed each building to rise or fall with the tides independently of the others. City Transportation was by powered Gondolas manned by Robot Gondoliers.

ROSEWOODS PLANTATION

One of the strongholds of the Red Conclave, although it isn't widely known as such. From the outside the plantation house looks luxurious. It was built with tan stones and decorated with white wooden carvings sometimes referred to in the construction trades as 'gingerbread'. Large octagon windows added to the overall look of the house. Similar housing for workers was scattered throughout the plantation.

The Plantation acreage is huge. Many fields of various crops were interspersed with large patches of forest left for native animals and plants. Cattle, goats, and sheep frolicked and loitered in the pastures. Passing through the various fields, ran well kept, dusty roads. Several barns provided shelter to livestock, along with various sheds which might have held tools or robot repair garages, a few were undoubtably Hermit Flyer coops, or lint dragon box hives. The boxes stood just behind the main buildings. A modern greenhouse stood to the side of the plantation house courtyard.

DANCING BEACH

The city of Dancing Beach was built at the edge of a lush rain forest, where the Parchester river met the southern Langstino Sea. It's main tourist attraction was the Whisps. (SEE Animals)

As befitted a tourist town, the city boasted lots of take-outs, sandwich bars and cafés, offering a plethora of culinary choices and those who feel hungry for something else can enjoy the beach, water sports, art galleries or one of the many other recreational venues.

TECH LEVEL

Technology level and education levels are high. Although they love the outward appearance of the Renaissance, the colonists are unwilling to give up modern conveniences. Many things on Barsoom are deceptive; servants are usually highly programed robots, air sleds have been designed to resemble horse-drawn carriages or birds of prey, robots harvest the crops and handle food preparations, Gondolas which traverse the waterways are powered by Gregor Crystals and controlled by robots.

Barsoom does a great deal of research on miniaturized robots (nanites) which it exports to earth under the cover of shell companies with satellite offices on earth.

*The name Barsoom which is used as the name of a colony in these books, BARSOOM(R) is a registered trademark of Edgar Rice Burroughs, Inc. And Used by Permission.

ABOUT THE AUTHOR

A writer of Fantasy and Science Fiction stories, Gail has received high praise for her beautifully interlaced, imaginative worlds. She populates her universes with vital and interesting characters, skillfully intertwining their everyday lives with world changing events.

An omnivorous reader, she was inspired by her son, also a writer, to finish some of the incomplete novels she had begun over the years. She is heavily involved in local art groups and fills her time reading, writing, painting in acrylics, and spending time with her husband of nearly 50 years.

Gail has a background in business and used this expertise to develop a series of pamphlets (lumped together under the title "The Modern Artist's Handbook) advising artists and authors about how to improve their bottom line by applying business practices to the development and sale of their work.

Currently her family is owned by two cats, a mischievous young cat called Mab (after the fairy queen of air and darkness) and a mellow Gray Princess named Moonstone. In the past, the family shared their home with many dogs, cats, and a Guinea Pig, all of whom have passed over the Rainbow Bridge. A recent major surgery on her stomach, a bout with breast cancer, and arthritis in her hands have slowed her down a little, but she continues to write and paint.

GAIL DALEY

www.gaildaley.com

A NOTE FROM GAIL

Thank you for reading this book. While each book was designed to be read without having read the prior volumes, Characters from prior books do appear in each story. This is the 2nd book to be set on Barsoom and the eighth book in the Outlawed Colony Series; If you would like to read the first book set on this colony, it's Heirs of Avalon.

https://books2read.com/u/3y1MYV

The story will continue with more books. I plan on writing at least three books set on each colony. Including this book, I now have two books set on Arcadia, Shangri-La and Barsoom. The Outlawed Colonies with ties to Laughing Mountain are:

- St. Antoni (4 books and two tie-ins with my Dystopian Earth series)
- Arcadia (2 Books)
- Shangri-La (2 books)
- Barsoom (2 books)
- Lemuria (1 book)
- Halcyon (1 book)

I often get asked why I write. The answer is simple. I write books I personally would like to read. While it's always a joy to find other readers who enjoy the stories I do, I'm aware my brand of writing won't please everyone. Please, write to me anyway. I'd love to hear from you. Gail@gaildaley.com

PLEASE REVIEW! Honest reviews are critical to all authors, but especially critical to Indie authors like me, so please take a few minutes to tell me what you think of my work. It would be much appreciated if you write a review and share it on the site where you purchased it. Reviews don't have to be long and analytical. Just say what you think as though chatting with a friend. On behalf of all Indie writers and publishers **PLEASE, ALWAYS WRITE A REVIEW** for any book you read or audiobook you listen to.

If you would like to know when my next books are coming out, please follow me on social media sites or sign up to receive E-mail notices, either through Books2Read:

https://books2read.com/author/gail-daley/subscribe/1/72820/

Or directly on my website:
https://gaildaley.com/Sign-Up-4-Newsletters.php

A copy of my privacy policy can be found on https://gaildaley.com/Privacy-Policy.php

GAME THEORY

The Revolution is Coming!

An Outlawed Colony Adventure!

On a distant colony, a young couple plays a deadly game to stop a  *rebellion and keep their newly adopted children safe.*

Mathias and Ivette are thrust into a deadly game to protect their newly adopted children from a growing rebellion. With their families divided, the young couple must keep their children sheltered and protect their home from an impending invasion. Mathias is further horrified to discover his older brother is in league with the rebels. Can he betray his brother to save his family and his colony?

If you enjoyed the thrill of being caught in the middle of a war in Marie Lu's Warcross, you'll be hooked by Mathias and Ivette's adventures in this suspenseful novel. Learn More:

https://books2read.com/u/mlLEkW

#

HEIRS OF AVALON

BARSOOM I
OUTLAWED COLONIES 2

ABOUT HEIRS OF AVALON

The theft Top Secret technology is the catalyst for a lab tech's murder and plunges two couples into a web of criminal activity on the colony

of Barsoom*, a hybrid of advanced technology and Renaissance Culture.

This edge-of-your-seat thriller is set on the mysterious colony of Barsoom, where robot-driven carriages run on exotic crystals and Airsleds resemble birds of prey. Nothing on the Colony of Barsoom is what it appears; the colony is a hybrid of advanced technology and Renaissance Culture and hides a sinister criminal underworld. Filled with danger, suspense, and adventure, this book will have you guessing until the very End and Beyond.

If you enjoyed the science fiction thriller "Ready Player One" by Ernest Cline, you would _love_ this book.

Learn More:

https://books2read.com/u/3y1MYV

The name Barsoom which is used as the name of a colony in these books, BARSOOM(R) is a registered trademark of Edgar Rice Burroughs, Inc. And Used by Permission.

APEX PREDATOR

LEMURIA 1
OUTLAWED COLONIES 3
ABOUT APEX PREDATOR

The first world discovered by the Laughing Mountain Scientists was a doozy. A fitting match for Homo Sapiens—the deadliest predator of all time—maybe.

If the native animals here don't get you, the plants just might.

A tough young guide leads a group of explorers to a mysterious structure on an alien world.

This fast-paced sci-fi thriller will keep you on the edge of your seat. Zach Tylor is young, tough, and broke so he agrees to lead a group of explorers to a mysterious abandoned city on an alien world. The Halivaara Wheel is an ancient and enigmatic structure hidden away on a far-off alien world for centuries.

Life is hard on the Outlawed Colony of Lemuria, where plants and animals are huge, aggressive, and deadly. Homo Sapiens are apex predators, but they may have met their match on this planet.

When he uncovers a dangerous conspiracy that threatens not only his home world, but all the Outlawed Colonies, Zach finds himself in a fight for his life.

. Learn More: https://books2read.com/u/4ELPxY

BABYLON SHATTERED

SHANGRI-LA 1
OUTLAWED COLONIES - 4
ABOUT BABYLON SHATTERED

Welcome to Shangri-la the planet of psychics and a utopia gone wrong. *This thrilling science-fiction mystery will keep you guessing until the very end!*

A Cozy Science-Fiction Mystery

This high-stakes science-fiction thriller offers a riveting read full of mystery and suspense.

Clemintine LaSalle finds herself in the middle of a dangerous conflict as a war looms between the Reformers and the Conservatives. When she steals her mother's Indentured Contract papers, she inadvertently gets a blackmail list too, and someone wants that list badly enough to frame her for the blackmailer's murder. Clemintine must use her psychic abilities and newfound information to protect her family and solve the mystery of the blackmailer's death. From the clues of a forgotten past to the secrets of a hidden present, Clemintine must use her wits and skills to navigate her way through a thrilling journey full of twists and turns.

If you enjoyed Neal Stephenson's *Snow Crash*, you'll love Babylon Shattered.

Learn   More: https://books2read.com/u/b5jz67

THE ARCADIAN WEB

ARCADIA II
OUTLAWED COLONIES 5
Return To Arcadia for A New Outlawed Colony Adventure!

A lone investigator finds himself in trouble up to his neck when he probes the disappearance of an old friend.

The illicit drug business followed man when he colonized new planets, creating deadly new drugs with new names like Love Potion.

Cosimo Bedingfeld's life has been filled with bad luck and trouble. As an undercover investigator for the HIVE, he's constantly hip deep in a pile of dung. When Cosimo is sent to investigate the murder of an old friend in the southern islands, he meets Abigail Trelawney, the 'Spider Girl' of Aranea plantation who raises

Marabunta, giant wasp-spiders for their webs.

Despite his past mistakes, Cosimo has a chance at happiness, but will he take it? Follow Cosimo's adventures on the planet Arcadia as he battles the illicit drug business and discovers the truth behind the disappearance of an old friend.

Learn More:

https://books2read.com/u/mezBOY

CLONED AMBITION

HALCYON 1
OUTLAWED COLONIES 6

Set in a future where clones are seen as second-class citizens and Normals are threatened by their own creation, Scarlet and her Mate Dagmar must fight for their own freedom and survival.

Scarlet was created to be the vessel for an aging actress's brain when she reached maturity. But when her creator dies before the transplant can take place, Scarlet is sold to a clone breeding farm, and only narrowly escapes a terrible fate to rejoin her mate Dagmar and his band of 'wild' clones.

If you enjoyed the suspense and adventure of The Hunger Games, then you'll be captivated by Scarlet's journey for freedom in this thrilling novel.

CITY OF DECEPTION - Barsoom 2
OUTLAWED COLONIES 8

Learn More:
https://books2read.com/u/mgRM1z

DAUGHTER OF

SHADOWS

SHANGRI-LA COLONY 1
OUTLAWED COLONIES 7

Identity, Danger and psychic intrigue collide

Dive deep into the mysteries of identity

Every Shadow has a story to tell

Secrets Are Dangerous—but Not Knowing the Truth Can Cost You Your Freedom...

Welcome to Shangri-la, a **planet of psychics and a utopia gone wrong.** *This thrilling science-fiction mystery will keep you guessing until the very end!*

The mysterious Psychic Colony of Shangri-La is home to many secrets, and Tracy Lucent is determined to solve them. After arriving with no memory of who she is, Tracy's only clue to her identity is a locket with her name engraved inside. With each passing day, Tracy struggles to unravel the threads of her past, but when there is an attempt to kidnap her which she narrowly escapes, she knows she can no longer ignore the mystery of her past. With danger lurking around every corner and secrets waiting to be uncovered, Tracy must uncover the truth of her identity before it is too late.

If you enjoyed the suspenseful journey of identity discovery in books like The Maze Runner and Divergent and the suspense of The Girl with the Dragon Tattoo, then you'll love the thrilling ride that is Daughter of Shadows.

Learn More:

https://books2read.com/u/bPwzrd

PALADIN

MAGI OF RULARI
TRILOGY - 3

ABOUT PALADIN

"An intriguing mixture of Fantasy and Science Fiction."

What happens when two highly technological civilizations bring their Artificial Intelligences to a planet where Magic works, and the A.I.s learn to use it?

Cadence knows the price of justice all too well. After surviving a massacre that took her parents from her, she must protect her teenage sisters. Cadence is determined to bring her parents' murderer to justice. But teens from both the human and Sekhmet races are disappearing and each race blames the other for it. The mysterious Harmony the artificial intelligence who should have helped her, is locked out of the Ley Lines of power by a spell.

Cadence must find the missing teens, regain her inheritance, and bring her uncle to justice. With secrets and powerful magic around every corner, Cadence must rely on her wits and courage to achieve her goals.

Readers who enjoyed the thrilling urban fantasy of Sarah J. Maas' Throne of Glass series, will be captivated by this action-packed magical adventure.

https://books2read.com/u/md7p1d

QUANTUM LIGHT

SPACE COLONY JOURNALS - 7
ABOUT QUANTUM LIGHT

A family of innocent botanists finds themselves thrust into the middle of a drug war on an alien planet.

This thrilling science fiction adventure follows a family of innocent botanists as they find themselves in the middle of a dangerous drug war on an alien planet. When Rupert, Aire, and Clan members Sesuna and teenage Selick, along with their companion, the Dactyl Pelcon, come to Trellya to negotiate the purchase of plants, they are unaware of the danger that awaits them. Teenage Selick wants to meet the birth mother who sold her to the Thieves Guild as an infant. Sesuna came to investigate suspicious activity on her family's Trellyan estates, only to find that they have been taken over by rebels planning to finance their revolution with the sale of Submit, an illegal, highly addictive drug. In a desperate attempt to save her family's lands, Sesuna, Selick, Rupert and Aire must face the dangerous leader of the rebels and defeat him.

If you enjoyed the suspenseful sci-fi novel "The Loyal League", you'll be sure to love this book too.

Learn More About these books:

https://books2read.com/ap/n41KK8/Gail-Daley31

COMING IN 2025

Soturi!
Book 1 Space Colony Journals the Next Generation

Lady Selick O'Teague *ni* s'Rudin is a pariah in one world and a respected member of a powerful family in another. With her unique half-blood

status, she has the perfect skillset to join Vensoog's security forces and put her training from the notorious Thieves Guild to use. But when she tags along with her Policewoman sister Lucinda and Private Eye Tom Draycott to meet a supposed recruiter for the Thieves Guild, she soon discovers that she may be in over her head.

This thrilling story of identity, loyalty, and family will have readers on the edge of their seats as Selick navigates the complicated worlds she inhabits.

CITY OF DECEPTION - Barsoom 2
OUTLAWED COLONIES 8

If you enjoyed the suspense and
intrigue of books like Neil Gaiman's
American Gods, you're sure to be on
the edge of your seat with *Soturi!*
Lady Selick O'Teague ni s'Rudin's
story.